THE SECOND TIME AROUND

A WILLOW BAY NOVEL

KELLY COLLINS

BOOK NOOK PRESS

ONE

C ould she leave someone behind but love them forever? That was a question Brie Watkins had pondered repeatedly. It was the fifth wedding anniversary she would celebrate without him. She poured wine and plated David's favorite meal of chicken cordon bleu. It wasn't the store-bought kind that came from the frozen section. This had been made from scratch. Digging deep into her soul, she found her inner Julia Child and prepared it from memory. She'd packed the cookbook with her other belongings, which were halfway to Willow Bay in the back of a moving van.

She walked around the empty house with a lump lodged in her throat. Today she would set out on a journey to test her theory about love and loss and heartache.

"I would have never left you or this place, but Aunt Em needs me." She should have felt self-conscious talking to David out loud, but it was like sleeping when she was tired or drinking a glass of water when she was thirsty. It felt totally natural.

Picking up her glass of wine, she stared at the picture of David. He always looked so handsome in his uniform. The army green shirt and jacket brought out the emerald of his eyes. Mischief danced there in the candlelight's glow. All she had left was her imagination. It was weird that she didn't smell the meal but his cologne.

She sat beside his chair at the folding table she'd borrowed from the neighbor and cut into the chicken; cheese oozed onto the paper plate.

"Aunt Em sounds good, and her spirits seem high." She took a bite and let the flavors settle over her tongue. The ham's saltiness and the cheese's richness should have blended perfectly, but the flavors fell flat. This year everything felt and tasted differently.

"I know it's the right thing to do, but it pains me to leave behind everything we built together."

She examined every detail of the dining room, from the crown molding to the hardwood floors they'd sanded by hand. Every dream they'd had was in the walnut stain and continental blue paint they'd chosen for the walls. She could almost hear the pitter-patter of feet from several planned Watkins's children. She sighed and blew out the candle.

Her friends and family thought she was crazy, having these anniversary dinners after David passed away, but these moments made her feel closer to him. But it was time to face reality: He wasn't in the cordon bleu or the wine. He wasn't in the dining room, the paint, or the floors. He'd been gone for years and wasn't coming back. Though she'd tried to hold on to him forever, it was like he was pushing her away and telling her to live her life. As much as she wanted to fight him, she knew he was right. It was time to move on.

She emptied her plate into the trash can, picked up his picture, and hugged it to her chest. It was almost as if she could feel his arms around her. He would always remain in her heart, but it was time to let the past go.

She cleaned up, returned the table and chairs to the accommo-dating neighbor, and packed the last of her belongings. She took one last look around before emptying the trash, locking up the house, and walking to her car, where she tucked the frame into the open box inside the trunk. After blowing him a kiss, she shut the trunk and climbed behind the wheel.

Taking her phone from her purse, she dialed Aunt Em, who picked up on the first ring.

"Are you on your way?" For a woman who was supposed to be sick, Aunt Em sounded pretty lively.

"I am."

"Shh," Aunt Em loudly hushed her friends. "She's on her way."

Brie could hear their muffled voices in the background. They called themselves the fireflies, but Brie thought of them more like busy bees. They swarmed everything and everyone and were a nuisance. And lord help you if you got on the tail end of their stinger. Aunt Em was the queen bee. Nothing happened in Willow Bay that she didn't know about. The town was her personal hive.

"What time do you think you'll get here?"

"It'll be really late. I figure it'll take me about six hours, which puts me there around eleven. Why? Is something wrong?"

Again, the phone was muffled, and there were a lot of giggles.

"I'm trying to figure out when the stripper arrives."

"You didn't hire a stripper."

"How would you know?"

"Because Marybeth would confess to the entire congregation on Sunday. She can't help herself. She feels responsible for every one of your souls."

It was true. Marybeth was the pastor's wife, but she wouldn't think twice about cheating at Bunco or a game of cards on

Saturday night as long as half of what she won ended up in the basket for the good Lord on Sunday. She was known for blurting out her sins and those of others to make up for a transgression.

Brie would never forget the time Aunt Em hired "entertainment" for Tilly's forty-fifth birthday. Marybeth had stood up during the gospel, raised her hands in the air, and asked the Lord to forgive Aunt Em's wicked ways and bless the naked man who'd danced for them the night before.

"Okay, no stripper, but there's a new carpenter in town. A lot is happening in Willow Bay these days."

"Don't tell me that. I want to come home, grab a book, an umbrella, and some sunshine."

"You can do that for the first few days, but then we'll be busy. It's Willow Bay's Centennial Celebration, and we've got the Spring Harbor Hop. I need your help."

Brie let out a groan that lasted at least five seconds. The Spring Harbor Hop meant hundreds of tourists would converge on the town and take up every square inch of the beach. She'd be lucky to find a ray of sunshine, much less an umbrella. She had to remind herself she wasn't coming back to vacation. Her goal was to help her aunt in her time of need. "You've got it. There will be time for fun and games later." She hoped so, anyway. Aunt Em was the last of her family and without her, she was alone.

"You there, sugar britches?"

Brie hadn't been called that in years. It was a nickname her aunt gave her because she always had some kind of candy smeared on her pants. "I'm here." Thinking about candy made her think about her friend Tiffany, who worked at the taffy shop in town. "Whatever happened to Taffy Tiff?"

"She's around. She owns the shop now. It's called Sweet on You. You'll be surprised at what's the same and what's changed."

Years ago, Brie had left Willow Bay and never looked back, but

4

family was family, and you didn't turn your back on them when they needed you. Aunt Em called and said she had the Big C and needed her.

"How are you feeling?"

Aunt Em sighed. "Oh, you know, sweetie. I'm meaner than a dog full of ticks."

"You getting enough rest?"

"I've got my regimen down. I wake up, get up, and grab my coffee, which I like with a little nip of whiskey. My sweet tea with a bit of Long Island, and my lemonade with a dab of vodka. At my age, they say it's important to thin the blood."

The way Aunt Em talked, one would think she was ancient, but she was only in her fifties and too young to worry about things like cancer. No one would think Brie had to worry about death either, but here she was, a widow at thirty-two. Life wasn't fair, but you had to keep living.

"Seriously, Aunt Em? Who is 'they'? What does the doctor say?"

She laughed. "He says I look fabulous for my age." There was a loud noise on Aunt Em's end. "I have to go, love. A guest is checking in—Charlotte, leave the poor man alone. He can carry his own luggage. I swear to the saints, woman, you need to stop eatin' those yams. Next, you'll be growing a full beard."

The phone went dead, and Brie laughed all the way to the state line.

LEAVING Louisiana and entering Texas shouldn't have been a big deal, but it was like moving from one country to the next. Her mama, bless her soul, always said Texas was its own place. It might have been part of the United States, but that seemed accidental.

Olivia Barron Brown believed the center of the universe started with Texas, and the rest of the country belonged to the Lone Star State.

Brie pulled into town and couldn't believe her eyes. So much had changed, and so much had stayed the same. She drove down Main Street smiling but with a heavy heart. The last time she visited, David had been alive, and so had her mother. The three of them had walked down the street, eating ice cream cones, and checking out the local antique store.

Back then, the town wasn't celebrating its centennial. The windows hadn't been adorned with red, white, and blue fabric banners. Planters hadn't been overflowing with flowers, and a man wasn't hanging from a light pole that curved over the street.

She slammed on her brakes when she heard the *thunk* of his ladder hit her car.

"Oh, Lord almighty." Her hand went to her heart. He was hanging like a banner in the wind. She hopped out of her car. "What are you doing on a ladder in the middle of the street so late at night?" she hollered. "I could have killed you."

"There's still a chance," he yelled, his legs dangling back and forth. "If you don't get my ladder, I'd say I'm about 2.8 seconds from breaking a leg. You think you can help a guy out?"

She was a handy girl, brought up on weekend projects and hard work, but she'd be damned if she could get her head to work straight at that moment. She looked up at the familiar face. "Cormac McClintock, is that you?" The last time she'd seen him, he'd also been hanging from a pole, but back then, he was wearing tighty-whities and knee-high socks. The bullies at the school had stripped him down and tied his skinny bean-pole body to the football goal post. "Last time I saw you—"

"Don't say it."

She picked up his ladder and maneuvered it under him. "You

seem to get yourself in the darnedest situations. Why are you up there, anyway?"

He climbed down and pointed to the festoon hanging from the light. "I have a lot of town pride."

"After what this town did to you?"

"It wasn't the town, just a select few. What about you? Why are you back?"

"Aunt Em needs me, with her not doing well."

"What's wrong with Em?"

"She's got..." This wasn't her story to tell. "... me back. She's got me back."

"It's just like old times," he said.

"Not really. So much has changed."

He smiled. "And so much is the same. Funny how we all come back to where we began."

"What do you mean?"

"Nothing. Just reminiscing about the past. You know, the way it used to be. I was thinking about past lives and past loves."

The only other man she'd loved was Carter Kessler. He'd been her first for everything—first kiss, first dance, first *first*. He'd also been the first boy to break her heart. She was a Brown, and he was a Kessler. It had been a disaster from the beginning. In these parts, they were like the Hatfields and McCoys.

If she ever ran into Carter Kessler, there would be fireworks, but they wouldn't be the kind bought in bulk from China and set off over the bay in celebration. Nope, these would be land mines, IEDs, hand grenade-lobbing fireworks. Carter Kessler had a lot to answer for, like why he'd left her at the altar all those years ago.

TWO

C arter Kessler had made a lot of mistakes in his life. The first was leaving Willow Bay, and the second was coming back. He sat on the porch of the dilapidated resort, drinking a beer and trying to put the pieces of his life together.

He stared past the railing to the big willow tree in the yard next door. It dripped under the weight of fairy lights, swaying in the gentle breeze. The air carried salty brine from the harbor and the soft buzz of cicadas nesting in the trees. A dozen years ago, he'd stood under that tree and kissed the woman of his dreams the night before their wedding. He walked her to her door and told her he'd be waiting for her the next day. That didn't happen.

"Is that you, Carter?" He turned his head to take in Em standing on the sidewalk with her arms filled with towels. Their properties intertwined with The Brown Resort's walkways meeting The Kessler Resort's at several points.

"Yes, ma'am. How are you?"

"I can't complain. You?"

He chuckled. "I could, but who would listen?" He wasn't back in Willow Bay by choice. He was there because his father died, and now he had a resort to sort out.

"Sorry about your father."

"Thank you for that."

"Some exciting stuff coming to town," she said.

"Oh, you mean the Harbor Hop and the Centennial Celebration?"

"That too." She glanced down at the towels in her arms. "I need to get these in the laundry. Tomorrow is going to be a busy one." She took a step forward and stopped. "I am really sorry about your father. He was never the same after..." She shrugged. "Everything." She disappeared into the darkness by the shrubs.

The mention of his father left him thinking about the night that changed everything. Cyrus Kessler had been married to his mother, Claudia, for twenty-five years. He didn't know anyone who had a more rock-solid marriage. Well, he knew of one, and that was Brie's parents, Benton and Olivia Brown. They'd been married a lifetime, too. You couldn't put the two families in the same room together, except for weddings, funerals, and Sunday church services. They were like combining oil and water. If they hadn't been the biggest rivals at the hottest Willow Bay resorts, they might have been best friends, but competition had a way of killing friendships.

That night, he'd searched high and low for his father because he needed reassurance from someone whose marriage he admired. He wanted what his parents had. He wanted twenty-five years of bliss. What he found changed his world forever. He'd entered the boathouse and found his father in the arms of Brie's mother. They didn't know he'd seen them, but he couldn't erase what was now etched into his memory. That betrayal rocked the foundation of everything he believed about marriage and loyalty and family. How was he supposed to stand in front of Brie the next morning when his father had been with her mother the night before? How was he supposed to tell her that her mother had betrayed her beloved father? She would never have believed him. He couldn't start a new life with the woman he loved when his was built on a rickety foundation of lies.

In Brie's eyes, her mother was an angel, and her father walked on water. They were pillars of the community and loved by all. Who was he to take that from her? He packed and left town because to stay meant he'd have to deal with the problem. If he wasn't mature enough at twenty to confront his father about sleeping with his future mother-in-law, he had no business getting married. He'd tried to protect everyone and ended up protecting no one. Two years later, his mother left his father for a builder in Florida. That was how Carter found his niche as a carpenter.

In the distance, a couple of kids snuck into the boathouse. "Damn it." He rolled to his feet and balanced his beer on the rail. It teetered, then tottered and fell to the sand. He dove, trying to catch it, but was too late. The sand swallowed the rest of his drink. "What a waste. The trip here might be just that." He wouldn't have cared that the kids were down there if he knew it was safe. Hell, he'd spent more than his fair share of evenings kissing Brie under the rafters, but the whole resort was a mess. Time had stood still for The Kessler Resort while everything else in Willow Bay moved on.

He got to the boathouse and opened the door. "You two need to come out." There were hushed whispers and then silence. "Hey, I know you're there. Come out now." His voice echoed off the walls. "It's not safe." There was no movement, so he did what he knew would have worked with Brie. "I saw black widows today. There seems to be a large infestation."

The girl squealed. Or maybe it was the guy. Seconds later, two heads popped up from one boat.

"Way to ruin the night, man," the teenage boy said. "What happened to the old dude? He wouldn't have cared we were here."

"The old dude is dead." Water slapped the boats and strained wood creaked as both teens stood staring.

"Wow, I didn't know. I'm sorry. Was he your dad?"

"Something like that." Carter hadn't spoken to his father since the night he left town. He never mentioned the betrayal. Everyone thought he'd gotten cold feet and ran. He was fairly certain his mother knew the truth, but they'd never talked about it. He wouldn't be here now if his father hadn't died and left him the resort. All he wanted was to clean it up, sell it, and leave again.

The kid helped his girl out of the boat and walked her to the door. "What are we supposed to do?"

Carter laughed. "I'm a believer in young love." He rolled his eyes, but he wasn't sure they could see it in the moonlight peeking through the open-beamed ceiling. Love didn't work out for him, but maybe it would for this kid. "Try taking her out to dinner or for a walk on the beach. Maybe take one of these boats out for a spin on the water. You can rent them, you know?" He leaned against a post that groaned under his weight. "Not mine, because I'm not even sure they'll stay afloat." He jutted his chin at the property next door. "I'm sure the Browns still rent theirs. When I was a kid, we used to take the paddle boats to the buoy and back."

"Too much work," the boy said.

"Well, love takes work. You put in the effort now, or you'll regret you didn't later." Like he had. He pointed to the door. "Don't let me catch you here again." He made a mental note to get a padlock for the door. After they shut it, he caught sight of the carved heart above the doorjamb. Inside it were the initials *C* and *B*.

He moved up the beach to the creaky deck, where he opened the cooler and grabbed another beer. Twisting off the cap, he sat back and took the first icy gulp. "What am I going to do with you?" He was talking to the property but also to himself because he'd been in limbo for years. He'd tried once to reconcile with Brie, but it had been a feeble attempt. She wasn't even aware he'd tracked her down. He'd come to his senses about a month after he deserted her, but it took him several more to devise a plan. His mother had all but called him an idiot, which he realized was true the day he left. But it took wallowing in self-pity and beer to realize the sins of the father weren't his.

He tracked her to Louisiana State University, prepared to beg and plead for forgiveness, but she was happy and dating a guy named David. Carter wouldn't ruin another happy ending for her, so he walked away. He imagined she was married and had a few children by now. Sometimes it was better not to know. Thinking about her was like picking at an old wound that had never healed. He tipped back his beer and swallowed years of regret. Though he wasn't happy about being back in Willow Bay, things could be worse. He could be looking into Brie's eyes and regretting every decision he'd ever made. Her absence made it easier to get in and get out and never look back.

Headlights next door made him scoot his chair deeper into the shadows. He'd been home for days but had stayed out of sight. Until he had a solid plan, he wanted to maintain a low profile. Most of the work the boathouse needed was cosmetic, which he could do himself, but there were a few structural fixes that needed to be done by professionals.

People said you shouldn't cross the same bridge twice, and he wondered if returning to Willow Bay was like putting his life on rerun, or if he was erasing his past and getting a chance at a redo.

None of the old players were around to mess up his game. His father was gone. His mother was happily remarried and living in Florida with Frank. Brie's mother and father had passed away. Even though Em was around, she'd never been a problem before so shouldn't pose one now. As far as he could tell, Brie had also evaporated. It would be easier than he imagined, making a new start of it here. Maybe selling the property wasn't the right choice.

A new arrival at The Brown Resort pulled forward too far and crushed the hedge. It was a constant problem and one that had driven his father crazy. Carter had told him a hundred times to line the drive with big rocks. All it would take was one boulder to the bumper and that would be the last time they'd make that mistake. The problem was, his father wouldn't have been that obvious. He'd have sprinkled nails or screws and made it look like negligence on the Browns' part, which was how the feud perpetuated.

The woman got out of her car and stretched.

Carter stood in the shadows and heard his father's voice leave his mouth. "Could you kindly pull your car off the shrubs?"

The woman leaned forward, peering into the dark. "Is that you, Mr. Kessler?" She moved from side to side. "It's me. Brie."

Shocked, he took a step back but didn't realize how close to the edge he was and fell off the deck.

"Mr. Kessler? Are you okay?"

No, he was not okay. His entire plan about a peaceful return to Willow Bay had just gone up in smoke.

She walked a few steps forward, but the door to The Brown Resort opened and Aunt Em stepped out.

"Brie Watkins, get over here and give me a hug."

Carter peeked above the edge of the decking.

"Who are you talking to?" Aunt Em asked.

Brie looked his direction as if she was staring straight at him. "I thought I was talking to Mr. Kessler, but he didn't answer."

"Well, of course not, honey. He died a few weeks back. Now come on in. Welcome home, baby. I have a feeling things are about to get exciting around here."

THREE

It felt good to be in Aunt Em's arms. She looked so much like her mama. It was almost like they were twins, only Em was two years younger and had honey-colored hair and eyes like a stormy sky, while her mother had darker hair and eyes the color of sapphires. A person had to see them to appreciate their beauty.

Brie breathed in the smell of home. The Brown Resort always smelled like apple pie and cinnamon, and it wasn't because of candles. It was because of Tilly's baked goods. She'd been with the resort for as long as Brie could remember. She wasn't a relative, but she might as well have been. She rushed from the kitchen, wiping her hands on a filthy white apron.

Brie barely had time to clear the door before Tilly tackled her like a linebacker, wrapped her in a hug, and spun her in circles until Aunt Em yelled, "Put Brie down."

"I can't help myself. I haven't seen her in years. Let me hug your neck, darlin'." Tilly grabbed Brie's shoulders and shook her like a change jar, hoping to dislodge a few dimes. "You haven't changed one bit." Brie grabbed hold of the front desk to stop the dizziness. Tilly didn't give her much time to recover before she pulled her in for a bear hug. She let go after several long seconds and took her hand and walked her into the kitchen. The older German woman was short, had short curls, and if Brie's memory served her correctly, a short temper. "I made all your favorites," she said. "Cinnamon rolls, Mexican wedding cookies, and rice crispy treats with rainbow confetti. I even made those disgusting no-bake cookies you love so much. You know, the ones with peanut butter, cocoa, and oats?" She made a blech sound and matched it with an equally disturbing look: lips pursed, nose scrunched, and eyes closed.

Brie didn't have the heart to tell her that her taste buds had matured since her last visit, and she couldn't stand those no-bake cookies anymore, but she'd smile and choke down a few because Tilly had made them.

"How long has it been?" Tilly asked.

Em cleared her throat and Tilly seemed to get smaller when she realized she'd brought up the worst year of Brie's life. But that short temper flared. "Don't be giving me a hard time. I've been here, and this one abandoned me years ago. While I want to hug you some more, I've more of a mind to turn you over my knee." Tilly poked her shoulder with a strong finger. "Never do that again."

"Yes, ma'am." As soon as the words were out, Tilly forgot about the whoopin' she wanted to give Brie, and instead pulled her in for another hug. Thoughts of her last visits played through her mind like a movie.

Brie had breezed through town a half-dozen years ago to see Mama and then five years ago to bury her. That had been a challenging year. David died from an IED, and Daddy had a heart attack. Mama died a few weeks later when she was hit by a drunk driver. She stayed long enough to touch the ground, do what she had to, and get out. There was too much hurt in Willow Bay—too much hurt in her short life. She wasn't sure if she'd ever open her heart again. Even though she didn't want to be here, she needed to buck up and find her spine because Em needed her.

Tilly set out teacups and put the kettle on to boil. It wasn't just any pot. It was a copper kettle that had belonged to Brie's mother and her mother before that. There was enough green on that pot to kill them all from some illness a person could get from drinking from copper, but no one had died from it yet, and if they had, well, there was no record of it. It was only used for special occasions, and her return counted.

While Tilly puttered around the kitchen, collecting everything from lemon wedges to the honeypot, Em and Brie took a seat by the window. This was the one part of the house where guests were not invited. It was an enormous two-story house that had been built over a hundred years ago. Brie liked her grandfather's telling of the story because it included pirates and treasures, but it had been a vacation home for a wealthy family with lots of children. The Brown family bought the estate when upscale family resort vacations took off, and it had been a vacation destination ever since.

The property contained the main house, which had ten rooms, and six separate bungalows. It hadn't always been that big. The Browns had taken over the land next to them. That caused a big stir in town because it made their property twice as big as The Kessler. Before then, Mr. Kessler made sure everyone knew that everything he had was bigger and better than anyone else's, but after the Browns' land purchase, he couldn't keep up. He was virtually locked in, with no place to expand. From that point forward, the Brown Resort was without a doubt, the biggest place to stay on Willow Bay.

"Are you sure Mr. Kessler died? Someone told me to move my

car." Brie looked out the window, but the Kessler property was dark.

"I can say with certainty that Cyrus Kessler is not at that house."

"He isn't, but—" Tilly had walked over, and Aunt Em stood and stepped on her toe. "Ouch." Tilly pushed her away. "What is wrong with you?"

Aunt Em gave her a look. It was one Brie knew well. It was a *you said too much* face, but there wasn't enough for her to decipher what was going on. She was also too tired to care.

"The water is boiling." Aunt Em measured loose leaf tea into strainer baskets before setting them into the pretty teacups on the table. "Cyrus passed a few weeks ago."

Brie continued with the subject because eventually whatever these two were up to would come out. "What about Claudia?"

"She left Cyrus ten years ago, remarried, and lives in Florida with her new husband, Frank."

Brie desperately wanted to ask about Carter but restrained herself because it was better not to unearth old skeletons. "Claudia left Cyrus?" That seemed impossible. They had been married forever, or for what seemed like an eternity. Like her parents, they'd been poster children for relationship goals. The marriages everyone strived to have. "I'm surprised. I thought they were happy."

Aunt Em sighed. "You were a kid. You only saw what people wanted you to see."

That statement puzzled her. "Not true. I saw everything."

Aunt Em smiled. "Did you?"

The pain of twelve years sliced straight through her. It was like a dull, rusty blade digging into her scarred heart and twisting slowly. "Obviously not. I had blind spots, or I would have seen that Carter didn't truly love me. That's water under the bridge." She'd married and had her happily ever after, so why did that betrayal still feel so raw and unfinished? It had to be because she was back in Willow Bay.

Brie picked up her tea, sipped, and let the bitterness roll over her tongue before reaching for the honey dipper and waiting for the golden goodness to drizzle inside the cup.

"That's the good clover honey I get from Cricket's Diner."

"Is she still there?" Ms. Cricket had to be at least seventy.

Aunt Em laughed. "She's made a deal with the devil or those bees—I'm not sure which—but she doesn't look a day over fifty. It's not fair."

Tilly finally sat. "Lots of things aren't fair."

"Yeah," Brie said. "Like Em getting cancer."

Tilly had just raised her teacup to her lips, but she dropped it. The fine bone China shattered on the floor. "Wait." She turned to Em. "You have cancer? Since when? Why didn't you tell me?" Tears sprang to the woman's eyes.

Brie stared at her aunt in utter disbelief. How could she not have shared that information with one of her closest friends? Em shifted in her seat like a convict awaiting sentencing. Something wasn't right. She thought about all the conversations she'd had with her, and they'd all ended with *I need you here.* There'd been urgency, but as she reflected, her aunt never spoke of her illness but that one time, when she said she had the Big C. "Wait a minute." She took several breaths, trying to get her racing heart under control. "You don't have cancer, do you?" A fiery thread coiled inside her belly. "I sold my house because you said you had the Big C."

She sipped her tea and swallowed hard, then added honey, and rather than wait for it to drip, she sunk the dipper straight into her tea. She stirred so vigorously it sloshed over the side.

Tilly rose and scooped up her broken cup, eyeing Em. "Maybe it's you I should turn over my knee. Let me get my wooden spoon."

"Now, girls, it's important you both calm down." Em stood and went to a kitchen cabinet, then grabbed a bottle of whiskey and a fresh cup for Tilly. When she returned, she uncorked it and took a big swig before pouring a shot into their cups. "Let's toast to Brie's return to Willow Bay."

Brie gawked at Em, who held her teacup up as if they were toasting to their health or the New Year. That fire in her stomach burned hotter. She leaned forward, so she was mere inches from her aunt. "Do you or do you not have cancer?"

"Would you like a cinnamon roll?" Em asked.

Brie sat back and crossed her arms. "You lied to me."

Tilly filled her teacup to the top with whiskey and did the same for Brie. "Did you tell her you had the C-word?" She tipped her cup back and drank it all in a few gulps.

Em breathed in and out like she was practicing for Lamaze classes. "I do have the C-word." She leaned over and pointed to her eyes. "Crow's feet. Don't you see them? I'm not getting any younger, and I can't run this place by myself."

Brie couldn't believe what she was hearing. She gulped down her whiskey and shoved her chair back so abruptly, it toppled over. "I jettisoned my life because you have crow's feet?"

"No, you did that because you needed to be here. I just gave you a reason to come back. This is your home. It's where you belong."

Brie paced the kitchen. "But I had a life."

"You didn't have a life. That ended the day David died. You were merely existing."

That little fire turned into a full, blazing inferno as the whiskey mixed with her anger. "I can't believe you. I gave up everything to come back to the last place I'd ever want to live because of you. You're the only person I trusted, and you lied to me." She flopped back into the seat.

"Brie, let me explain."

Her head was spinning. Maybe the equivalent of three shots of whiskey on a mostly-empty stomach wasn't a wise choice. "What's there to explain? Just tell me where I'm sleeping tonight."

"Can't we talk this over?"

"No. I need to think, and I'm feeling tipsy already." She pointed to the bottle. "What proof is that?"

Tilly smiled. "It's the good stuff."

"I deserve something good after this betrayal." Brie picked up the bottle of whiskey. "Which bungalow is mine?"

Em sighed. "You're in number three. It's the only one we have open."

Brie marched to the front door.

Tilly asked, "Should we tell her?"

Brie held up a hand. "I've had quite enough surprises tonight." She uncorked the bottle and took several swigs before capping it. Pointing at her aunt, she yelled, "You and I will hash this out tomorrow, but right now, I'm going to bed." She marched out the door and down the steps to her car, where she opened her trunk and tugged her suitcase out. That's when she remembered she'd driven over the hedges. She got in the car and backed up. When she exited, she stared at the dark building. Not a soul was in sight. She was positive she had heard voices. Someone had been there. She lugged her suitcase down the sidewalk and past the building but stopped, and out of spite, yelled, "I moved my car. Are you happy?"

"Thank you, Brie. I appreciate the kindness."

She'd never expected to hear that deep voice again and nearly fell over. "Carter Kessler, is that you?"

FOUR

Carter came out of the shadows. He figured it was time to rip this Band-Aid off. He'd been peeling Brie Brown away from him for years, and no matter what corner he tugged at or how slowly he tried to do it, it was always painful. "Carter Kessler, in the flesh."

"Why were you lurking there? Were you too scared to face me?"

She stumbled off the uneven plank walkway into the sand, taking her suitcase and bottle of whiskey with her. She looked at the bottle as if she didn't recognize it. She pulled it closer to scrutinize, then she swirled the contents before uncorking it and taking several gulps. Wincing after each swallow, she recapped the bottle and hugged it. "Stay right where you are, mister. What I have to say to you doesn't require me to see your pretty face."

"You think it's pretty, huh?" He always thought she was pretty, but he'd rather she found him handsome or cute, like a puppy. In this moment, he'd take pretty. He'd take anything that started a civil conversation with her. A few minutes ago, he'd been hiding behind his deck; anything was better than that.

A breeze blew off the bay, catching her hair. It carried it into her mouth, and she spat and sputtered and waved her arm around until she stumbled and fell on her bottom in the sand. She looked at her suitcase, which was next to her. "Nothing is going right today. Not even my cheesy chicken tasted good."

He moved forward a few feet. "Do you need some help?"

She pointed at him. "I told you to stay put. Haven't you caused enough trouble?"

He leaned against the pillar of his porch. "Looks to me like you're in trouble of your own making. Since when do you drink whiskey?" The Brie he knew didn't imbibe hard alcohol. She was more of a wine cooler or spritzer kind of girl.

"It's Em's."

"Oh well, that makes sense. She always liked the hard stuff."

"She did? It doesn't matter. The point is you don't matter. You being here doesn't matter. Just so you know, we will never be friends, and I will always hate you."

"Fair enough." He couldn't blame her. What he'd done was unforgivable, even if his motives had been genuine and aimed at saving her a world of hurt. He figured she'd move on, and she had.

She leaned on the suitcase. Even in the moonlight, and despite her frown, she still had the most beautiful blue eyes. Eyes as blue as the bay. The Texas coast wasn't known for its clear waters. It didn't have the blue of the Caribbean, but the way the reef protected the shore gave it a unique environment, and it had the bluest water. He'd forgotten how he'd thought of the bay as Brie blue, and paired with her chestnut hair, she was one of the prettiest girls in Texas.

He started back to the porch and his beer, but he caught sight

23

of her out of the corner of his eye, trying to stand. She stumbled over the suitcase and fell on top of it.

He raced toward her. "How much of that bottle did you drink?"

She looked at it and shrugged. "Not sure. Four or five."

"Four or five what? Sips? Gulps? Gallons?" She rose and tottered back and forth. Her back end was high in the air. All these years later, she still had the finest derriere he'd ever seen. "Let me help before you hurt yourself."

She wagged a finger behind her. "Stay away from me." She shifted and grunted and righted her suitcase, only to lose her balance again. This time she landed on top of it like it was a lounger. She squeaked, then smiled and let out an "Oh, this isn't so bad." She opened the bottle for another drink.

"Is that wise?"

"What do you care?" She laid back and looked up at the twinkling lights of the willow tree. "Did you know when I woke that morning, Mama got me ready? She used an entire can of Aqua Net. I smelled like Ms. Cricket but looked like Miss America." She ran her hands through her hair and sighed. "I had the prettiest braids going in every direction, but they all came together in the back." The whiskey bottle fell into the sand, which was probably a good thing. "So pretty."

"You were always beautiful, Brie."

"Oh, what would you know? You didn't even show up." She blindly searched around for the bottle but gave up quickly.

He sat a few feet away from her. He had a lot to say, but all he'd do was listen.

"You know what the funniest thing of all was?"

"Tell me." He scooped up sand and let it sift through his fingers. It kind of felt like how life was. It just got away from you.

"Mama wanted me to wear those fancy jeweled shoes. Those

heels were four inches high and pinched my toes. I'm telling you, she had me practicing for days, and I was in pure agony. I refused to wear them and hid them at Tiff's house, because I knew with the humidity, my feet would swell, and I wanted to dance under this tree with you. I didn't want to have achy feet on my wedding day, so I bedazzled my Keds. I had the perfect shoes for running, and I wasn't the one who ran." She turned on her side, showing her back to him.

He thought about how he'd apologize. He wasn't sure what she knew or didn't know. It had been so long, and both her parents were gone. Did she know her mother had been unfaithful? Did she believe until their dying days that they'd been hopelessly devoted to one another? Her father had died of a heart attack on a yacht filled with half-naked drunk coeds. Though he'd been gone, gossip traveled fast, and he'd gotten the condensed version every time his mother talked to someone from town.

"Look, Brie, I did what I did for a lot of reasons, but mostly it was to spare you pain and embarrassment."

"Mm-hm."

This was going far better than expected. "I'm sorry for hurting you, but if you'd known what I did, you would have been hurt so much more. I was a coward for many reasons. I should have stayed and let the grenade explode. At least then, maybe we could have worked it out, but I didn't have the maturity to face them or you." A loud sound startled him, and he scooted closer. "Brie." He reached out and touched her leg, only to realize she was snoring.

"Five more minutes, David. Just five more minutes."

"Great." Carter stood, brushed sand off his pants, and looked around. "What am I supposed to do with you?" The beach was empty, and the lights were out at The Brown Resort. His only choice was to use deduction. He'd seen the comings and goings at the resort the last few days. They were packed solid because of the

Centennial Celebration and upcoming Harbor Hop. His father had picked a terrible time to die. Not that The Kessler would have been ready, anyway. He didn't know what his father had been up to the last dozen years, but it wasn't taking care of the property.

He looked at the six bungalows on the Browns' estate. Numbers one and two were lit from inside, and numbers four, five, and six had cars in the driveways. The only place that looked unoccupied was bungalow three, and that was because the roof leaked. One look at the shingles told him that, so bungalow three it was.

"Let's go." He scooped her up in his arms. She weighed little. In fact, he would have guessed she weighed less now than she had when she was twenty, and he didn't like that. Women should have some curves. What had happened to hers?

She still wore the same perfume she had back then. It smelled like lilacs and summer, and he inhaled her scent. God, he had missed her. This should have been his life—walks on the beach and long, endless nights of making love—but he wasn't the man he'd needed to be back then. He should have stood up to his father and told her the truth.

Arriving at bungalow three, he opened the door. Still carrying her, he moved through the living room, straight to the bedroom, where he laid her down. After pulling the duvet to her shoulders, she gripped the edge of the blanket, and he noticed her wedding ring. All this time he hadn't thought about her husband, David. Where was he? The last he'd heard, they were married and living in Louisiana.

"David," she murmured, grabbing his hand, and bringing it to her chest. "It's cold."

Carter jerked away and tucked another blanket around her shoulders. "Sleep well, Brie." He went outside, moved the suitcase into the entry, and closed the door.

Nothing had changed for him at Willow Bay. There was still no future. Brie might be back, but what they had was in the past. She still had a husband, and they had a future together. For a second, seeing her again made him think anything was possible, but standing outside her door, he had to face reality. All he had was a run-down resort and a list of regrets. The best thing to do was fix the place, sell it, and put Willow Bay in his rearview mirror for good.

He walked toward The Kessler Resort and found the half-full bottle of whiskey Brie had left behind in the sand. "Waste not, want not," he said and picked it up.

"You gonna share that?" Em was sitting on his deck.

"What are you doing here?"

"I need to hire a carpenter."

FIVE

Brie woke to pounding. It was right above her head like someone was taking a hammer to her temple. *Bam bam bam.* She sat up and grabbed her aching melon. "Please stop the noise." Falling back, she covered her face with the pillow. The night before replayed on fast forward, like a major motion picture with surround sound. There was the trip, the tea, the ten-year-old whiskey, and Aunt Em's treason.

The hammering continued, as did her headache, and she threw her pillow at the ceiling, which came back and smacked her in the face. Swatting it away, she called, "Don't make me come up there, because I will." The last time she'd seen Hugh, he was close to eighty, and it took him thirty minutes to climb a ladder to change a lightbulb. She couldn't believe he was on the roof. She should be more forgiving of the feeble man, but she was in pain, and that trumped compassion. If he was on that roof, hammering away, she'd push him off to shut him up. "Hugh, if you don't stop that racket, I'm going to cause you bodily harm." Looking at the clock on the nightstand, she figured she'd use the early hour as her excuse to complain some more, but it was after ten, so she didn't have a plausible reason to continue ranting.

The noise ceased, and she said a silent prayer to God and thanked Him and her mama. This had Olivia Barron Brown's name all over it because she understood the benefits of beauty sleep after a bender. She had to be whispering in the Almighty's ear, telling him to stop the crazy long enough for Brie to get a cup of chicory-laced coffee, two painkillers, and one of Tilly's cinnamon rolls.

She kicked off the blankets and let her feet dangle over the edge of the bed. "What in the world?" She was still wearing her shoes. Even in her drunkest state, she'd never gone to bed in shoes, and then she remembered the beach and the sand and the suitcase and... Carter Kessler. She hopped off the bed and hit the ground running, which was probably more Hugh's speed, with her massive hangover.

Brie was barely out the door when a deep, sexy voice came from above. "Sorry to wake you."

She looked up, and there he was, wrapped in the sun's glow, looking like an angel. But she knew better. Carter Kessler was the devil incarnate. She pointed. "You stay away from me." She marched to the main building, where her aunt was behind the front desk, looking as chipper and happy as a pig in sunshine.

"We need to talk," Brie said as she went past, heading straight for the kitchen and a cinnamon roll, or maybe twenty.

Tilly was busy, so Brie went to the table and sat. The only thing left to eat was the no-bake cookies, but beggars couldn't be choosers, so she popped one in her mouth.

"I can't believe you love those," Tilly said.

"I don't. I find them repulsive, but they're the only thing here."

Tilly poured two cups of coffee, pulled a tray of cinnamon rolls from a rack in the corner, and joined Brie. "How about one of these instead?" She picked up the plate of cookies and tossed them in the trash can. "Let's pretend we never made or ate them."

"Deal." Brie breathed in the steam from her Louisiana coffee with chicory. Few carried it, but The Brown Resort did. You either loved it or loathed it. Brie loved it. "Why'd she do it?"

Tilly wiped her hands on her apron. "Because she loves you."

"Did anyone know she was bamboozling me to come back?"

"None of us did, so don't be gettin' mad at Marybeth or Charlotte. No one knew what she was up to. You know your aunt. She does what she wants."

Brie let out a sigh that everyone at the beach could probably hear. "I don't know if this is forgivable. I sold my house." She dug into the gooey cinnamon roll. "I had memories—David was there."

Tilly was silent for a second. It was one of those thoughtful pauses that said so much. "Honey, David is gone, and Em was making a point. The only one who refused to acknowledge he wasn't there was you. You were still sitting down to dinner with him."

It might have been true, but it felt invasive, as if they'd been peeking in her windows or her walls had been talking and had a direct line to her aunt's ear. "She's such a meddler." She glanced outside and glimpsed Carter. She hadn't gotten a good look at him last night. She'd only seen him in the shadows or in a haze of too much whiskey. Hell, in her inebriated state, she'd halfway thought he was a dream. Scratch that ... he was a nightmare. But she had to admit that time had been kind to him. He was still as handsome as ever. All those wishes he'd turn into a toad or grow warts or contract some necrotizing skin bacteria that would eat off those beautiful lips hadn't come true. No matter how much she'd wanted his thick sandy-blond locks of hair to fall out, it hadn't happened. Those broad shoulders hadn't Quasimodo'd either.

He leaned against the porch rail, gazing at the beach, looking better than he had a dozen years ago. The few silver hairs catching the sunlight made him look distinguished, not old. He was so tall; she was sure he regularly hit his head on the gingerbread trim that needed a good sanding and coat of paint. "Was he part of Em's grand scheme?"

Tilly gasped. "Heavens no. Can you imagine?" She sipped her coffee. "That would mean your aunt would be responsible for murdering Cyrus to get Carter back in town. You have quite the imagination, young lady. That's just a co-inky dink."

"I wouldn't put it past her." She pulled her cinnamon roll apart to get to the center, where the sweetest, sugariest, butteriest parts were. When a girl didn't shower and was still in yesterday's clothes, underwear, and mascara, she needed all the carbs she could stuff in her mouth. "Is this the first time he's been here?"

"Girl," Tilly said, "he hasn't been back since that day."

"No way." She didn't want to stare at the man, but she couldn't help herself. She believed everyone had a serial killer inside that was waiting to be freed, and hers had a thousand ways she wanted to torture Carter. "He disappeared. What the hell happened to him? One minute he was kissing me under that tree, telling me he was the happiest man ever, and then *poof*, he was gone. Who does that and why?"

Tilly licked her fingers, making an awful sucking sound before she wiped them on her apron. "I'd say that boy owes you some answers."

"Lots of people owe me answers. I think I'll start with Em and why she told me she had cancer."

Tilly stood. "In her defense, did she actually say the word cancer?"

Brie wagged her finger. "You don't get to defend her. When people say the Big C, they aren't talking about crow's feet."

The kitchen door opened, and in walked two women, followed

by Em. It irked Brie because they were supposed to hash things out in private, and Em brought protection. She had no beef with her aunt's friends. They were both angels, but her aunt sported horns and carried a pitchfork.

"Brie Watkins, get over here and give your Aunt Marybeth some love." Marybeth wasn't her real aunt, but she was close enough. Dressed in her Sunday best, she never left the house not perfectly arranged no matter what day it was. She would have made any southern mama proud, from her long blonde locks to her legs for days. Marybeth wouldn't be caught dead in trousers. She always said the good Lord gave her fabulous legs, and Chanel gave her dresses. It was a match made in heaven.

After a long hug, she let Charlotte have a turn.

"You're a mess." Charlotte frowned. "What are you wearing?" She never minced words. She moved around Brie like she was her next project, and she probably was. "You're too skinny. Your skin is sallow, and"—she stood back and looked her up and down—"are you wearing yesterday's clothes?"

Brie shoved her hands in her jean pockets and lowered her head. "How could you know that?"

Charlotte thumbed Brie's chin up and pointed to the button on her collar. "It left a mark on your face that probably won't leave until next week. Oh, honey." She licked a finger and wiped under Brie's eyes. "Did you know you age eight days for every one you don't wash off the makeup?"

Brie rolled her eyes so hard, she was sure she detached a retina. "Then I'd look two hundred and forty-six years old by now."

Charlotte grimaced. "Don't make me say it. I don't want to hurt your feelings."

"Girls," Em said. "Have a seat, and Tilly will make more

coffee." She laid her hands on Brie's shoulders. "Are you going to forgive me?"

Marybeth moved in like a hawk after prey or, in her case, after prayer. "I went to church this morning and talked directly to God, and I told him how sorry you were for lying to our Brie, and I swear,"—she raised her hands in the air—"my lips to God's ears, or in this case, my ears to God's lips, he said you were forgiven."

Charlotte leaned over and touched the corners of Em's eyes. "I've got some cream for that."

Even if Brie took Carter out of the equation, there was no way she'd survive in Willow Bay, but what other choice did she have? "I'm going to shower." She went around the table and hugged each of them like she hadn't seen them in a lifetime, which she hadn't. When she got to her aunt, she hugged her extra tight, like she wanted to squeeze the life out of her, but she figured it wasn't wise to have three witnesses to a murder and settled on a death glare. "Don't think for a second you're off the hook because you called in reinforcements. I'll meet you at Cricket's for dinner at six."

As she left, she lifted a hand to the fireflies. "I'll see you around, ladies."

Marybeth said, "You bet your sweet britches, honey. We're like lint on tape. You can't get rid of us that easy."

Accepting this was her life for the foreseeable future, she'd stay until she formulated a plan.

SIX

The problem with overwhelming projects was exactly that—
they were overwhelming. The condition of The Kessler
Resort meant Carter couldn't whip it into shape in a day. Standing
in the entryway, he stared at the decor which reminded him of
something he'd seen in the musical *South Pacific,* a movie his
mother had made him suffer through every year. He said he
suffered, but deep inside he loved it because he was a hopeless
romantic.

The Kessler Resort was a cross between an island retreat and a
southern plantation house. Inside there was the palm tree motif his
mother loved, mixed with the dark hardwood floors and pineapple
decor, which his father insisted on as a sign of hospitality. But it
was currently less than hospitable. Had a tsunami or dust funnel
blown through town and targeted only this property? Everything
to the left and right appeared unscathed, but it seemed like life had
moved around The Kessler Resort for years.

He probably shouldn't have spent the morning fixing the roof
of bungalow three, but guilt over Brie ate at him. While she

seemed to have landed on her feet, he knew he'd broken her heart all those years ago, so when Em had shown up on his patio last night, asking for a drink and a favor, he couldn't say no. Besides, she'd offered to pay him, and he never turned down money. Cyrus Kessler had been land rich but cash poor. His dad had owned the resort free and clear but had only a few grand in his savings account. Carter had used it to pay off Dobson's Funeral Home when his father died.

Dust and cobwebs hung from every corner of what had once been a beautiful entryway. It would take him days to clean. Forget about the white-glove treatment his mother would have expected when she'd run the place. But since he didn't have people skills, he wasn't interested in running a resort. He was more of a hammer and nails, behind-the-scenes guy. The handyman who could make it all work with a few boards and a roll of wire. He was the guy who'd get another ten years from a furnace everyone thought was dead. He'd never be the person who stood behind the front desk with a fake smile, who said, "Welcome to The Kessler Resort." That was his father, the schmoozer. Cyrus Kessler had been as slick as a fifties comb-over but lost his touch over the years. Maybe he was more like Samson. Carter never figured out if Samson's weakness was his hair or Delilah. Had his father's weakness been Olivia or Carter's mother?

"What the hell happened to this place?" He walked the perimeter of the room.

"Sad, right?" Em said from just outside the screen door.

Carter jumped six inches, and when he landed, a cloud of dust billowed around his boots. "Why are you lurking everywhere? And where is Brie?"

"After a few hours on the beach, I imagine Brie's getting ready for dinner tonight, and I'm not lurking. I was... okay, I was lurking." She opened the door, and the hinges complained so loudly, he was tempted to plug his ears. "I can send Hugh over to oil that. If he starts this way now, he may get here by supper."

"Why do you keep him on your payroll if he can't keep up?"

Em moved through the lobby like a cat hunting a mouse. "Because you don't toss people aside. When you're twenty, you don't understand that, but when you're my age, you see the value in people. Hugh has earned his place."

Was she talking about him and his father? "You don't know what Cyrus did?"

"You'd be surprised what I know." She ran a hand across the front desk. "The whole situation is a tragedy. There are a lot of victims here. You and Brie"—she shook her head—"that was the worst, but what are we to do?" She straightened a picture on the wall. "Are you keeping it or selling?"

He was dead set on selling until right that second. To say it out loud made his heart ache. The resort had been in the family for as long as he could remember. It was the only place he'd ever felt like he belonged. After leaving, he'd been a leaf in the wind, moving where the breeze took him. "Why? Do you want to buy it?"

Em laughed. "Are you kidding me? I can't keep up with what I've got going on at my place. I'm not getting any younger, and if you haven't noticed, there isn't a Mr. Brown at my side, helping me manage things."

Carter chuckled. The Brown women were not known for their subtlety. "I'm not sure about a Mr. Brown, but I bet Mr. Right is out there waiting."

"Aren't you sweet?" She reached up and pinched his cheek. "Maybe he's like Hugh. Let's hope he gets here before I die, or he does. Anyway, I have a proposition for you. Take a walk with me." Before he could say no, she opened the front desk cabinet, retrieved the master key, and trotted down the hall. "Your father didn't open during the last year. I don't think his heart was in it.

When your mother left, he slowed down a lot, but when my sister died, a piece of him did too."

"You obviously know, but does Brie?"

"No. I think you and I are it. But since your mother left him, I imagine she must have known." Em unlocked the first door on the right. "I always thought you had nicer rooms. Your mother had excellent taste in décor." She dragged her fingers through the dust, then walked to the bed and pulled back the duvet. "It will take a lot of man-hours to get this place in shape. It needs a thorough cleaning, and all the linens need changing."

"What are you talking about? In shape for what?"

"I want to sublease your ground floor." She went to the window and yanked open the curtains, sending dust motes into the air. "With the Centennial Celebration and the Harbor Hop happening, I'm getting ten calls a day for rooms I don't have. You have ten rooms and no guests. Seems like a win-win if you ask me."

"I also don't have a staff, nor do I want to manage one. I can barely microwave a can of chili." The room was filthy, and he supposed the rest of them were too. "Have you looked at the state my resort is in?"

Em nodded. "It's atrocious, but it's all superficial and nothing a little elbow grease can't take care of."

"Don't you make enough money?"

"This isn't about me. It's about Brie. Hell, maybe you can sell her the resort. She's relocating, and I'd love to have her living next door." As if the thought had just occurred to her, she clapped her hands in delight. "That's an amazing idea. I'll sublease the rooms from you, and Brie can manage them for the summer. How does that sound?"

Carter looked at her like she was a three-headed dog—with rabies. "Like you've lost your mind. In what world do you think I'd want my ex-fiancée working under my roof? That sounds about as pleasant as getting stung by a hundred murder hornets and falling into a vat of rubbing alcohol. By the way, where is her husband?"

She went into the bathroom and turned on the faucets, which spit and sputtered before running smoothly. That they worked at all surprised him. She pulled the towels off the racks and tossed them onto the bed. "Everything needs to be laundered."

"Uh-huh." He was still focused on Brie. "It's been twelve years. I heard she was engaged and figured she eventually married and had kids. No?"

Em's lips drew into a thin line. "Don't you worry none. Brie isn't a runner."

"Hey, I didn't see a choice. I either ruined how she was going to view marriage or how she saw her parents, and I refused to ruin how she saw life, so I left."

"That was a mighty big choice you made for her."

"I was an idiot, and I tracked her down to beg her forgiveness, but by then, she was already with someone named David. Did she marry him?"

"She did, and they were happy."

Were. "Why the past tense? I swear, if he mistreated Brie, I'll kill him."

"He was good to her."

Was. His hands curled into fists. "Stop it, Em. Either he's good to her or he isn't."

"David died five years ago in Afghanistan. She's a widow. I lied to get her to come home. Now I have to do something so she won't leave. Brie needs a project, and your resort is perfect. So, what do you say? Can I sublease the property? I need the space, and you can use the money to fix up the resort. What you do with it after that is up to you, but this one time, I'd encourage you to decide with your adult brain."

"Ouch." Her insult was painful but not unwarranted. "What

about Brie? What does she get out of all of this?" She hadn't been all that happy to see him.

"You were an unexpected coincidence I'm fairly certain she thinks I set up. While I'm adept at many things, I'm not capable of offing your father, bringing you back to Willow Bay, finding a buyer for her house, and getting her here in record time. I believe the universe is righting a wrong that happened a dozen years ago. The question is, Carter Kessler, are you going to help me set it straight or work against me and screw it all up again?"

That was the trillion-dollar question. Yesterday he was ready to move on. In his mind, Brie was in his past. Finding out she was a widow made a future possible. "When do you need the rooms ready?"

"Next week." She smiled. "I'll send over a crew tomorrow. All you have to do is say yes."

Could he erase twelve years with a single word? That was impossible. He couldn't bring back his father or Brie's parents. He couldn't mend the rifts in their marriages, nor should it have been his job. At least there was finally someone who knew what had happened. What was going on under their noses. Someone who might have more answers than he did. "How long had their affair been going on?"

"That might have been a good question to ask that night."

"I should have asked a lot of questions, but I only saw a single path."

"A path to ruin?" She shrugged. "You want to know the truth?"

"I think I deserve it."

"They were the first Kessler and Brown to fall in love under that willow tree. Olivia was about twelve, and your father was fourteen, and my mother, Bessy Brown, took a switch from that tree and blistered Olivia's bottom good for stealing a kiss. That first kiss was all it took for Cyrus to fall in love. There's magic in our lips." She puckered hers and blew a kiss into the air. "There's also an unwritten rule about our families not being allowed to fall in love, and it's passed through two generations. Olivia tried to break it with Brie, but she messed it up." They left the room, returned to the front desk, and Em put the key on the counter. "It's up to you. I'll take care of rooms and housekeeping and split what I bring in."

"What about food and amenities? I'm not sure if the boats even float. As far as I know, nothing around here works but the plumbing."

She smiled. "Plumbing is important. Outside of that, all I need are the rooms. I'll take care of the rest."

"Let's get back to Brie."

"I'll take care of her, too. She has a big forgiving heart, and that can work in our favor. Just tell me one thing. Do you still love her?"

"I never stopped." As if everything had been decided, Em left without further discussion, and Carter contemplated all the things that could go wrong with this arrangement.

SEVEN

"**W**ell, fry my feet and call 'em drumsticks. Is that you, Brie?"

She'd barely had enough time to take in the black, red, and white checker and rooster decor before Cricket O'Connor rushed forward and gave her a bear hug that pushed the air out of her lungs.

Brie wasn't sure what Cricket's real name was, but everyone called her that because of the clicking sound she made in her mouth. It wasn't a cluck or a tsk but more like the chirp of the bug. "You haven't aged a day." Aunt Em was right when she said the older woman must have made a deal with the devil because her skin was as smooth as a baby's bottom. "Have you been using Charlotte's creams and serums? You could pass for forty." It was only a slight exaggeration; Cricket could easily pass for Oprah's twin sister. Sweet talk could only help; Brie ordered pie, and she wanted a gigantic piece.

Cricket grinned. "I guess you want ice cream with that?"

Brie nodded. "Double scoop, please."

"That's some serious stuff if you need two scoops."

"I'd order a gallon if I thought you'd give it to me."

Cricket pointed to the corner booth. "Is anyone coming to help you swallow your sorrows?"

Brie slid into the booth, where a picture of a rooster glared at her with a caption that read, *I may look calm, but in my head, I've pecked you three times.* "I'm meeting Aunt Em at six, but she's the source of my woes." Brie took the spoon and fork from the place setting and slid the knife to the edge of the table. "Maybe you should hide the cutlery."

Cricket looked at her watch, which was nearly the size of a coffee saucer. "We've got a few minutes. You want to give me the condensed version?" She plopped into the booth across from Brie. "Condensed, because I'm old and don't have time for long stories, and it's dinnertime, and there are orders to take."

Brie hadn't seen Cricket in over a decade, so she wasn't sure where to start, but small towns spread rumors like hookers spread disease, so she skipped all the sordid details and went straight to yesterday.

"I sold my house, and I'm back, but so is Carter."

Cricket looked as if she was waiting for the punch line. "And?"

"Don't you get it? That's a problem."

She kicked her feet up on the bench seat next to Brie. There was nothing special about her high-top Converse until Brie saw that someone had drawn a middle finger on the soles.

"Is that what I think it is?"

She pulled down her foot and laughed. "You weren't supposed to see that. It's for my less than nice customers.

"Cricket O'Connor, you do not flip off your customers when they aren't nice."

The older woman's jaw dropped. "I would never. My right shoe does it as I usher them out. Let's get back to the non-problem

42

at hand. You're back, and so is Carter. This is your home. It's his home too, and all kids come home. It's where your roots are. You know his daddy just died, so of course, he'd return. And you ... I heard about your husband. Em mentioned something when she picked up that honey for you the other day. She was being nice, getting it for you."

"You're all in cahoots."

"In cahoots to what?"

"Did you not hear me? Carter and I are neighbors, for crying out loud. Have you seen him?" Brie whistled. "No matter how many plagues I wished upon that man, he ended up on the good side of everything."

"It sounds to me like you're the only one who is up to something."

"Me?"

She laughed. "You're here. He's here. What will you two do about that?"

"Absolutely nothing."

Cricket stood. "Seems to me you've got more on your mind than helping your poor aunt."

"Don't tell me Em told you she has the Big C too."

She let out a whoop that silenced the diner for a split second. "Is she complaining about those crow's feet again? I told her to use the honey. Bees are nature's miracle workers."

"I can't believe you two are colluding like that. I've got my eye on you both."

"You're watching me? You should check yourself, sweet cheeks. Poor Carter is trying to get his life straight, with his father just passing away and that resort being in such poor shape, and all you can think about is yourself and how good he looks. You should be ashamed."

"What are you talking about?"

She pulled a pad and pen from her back pocket. "Would you like a meal first, or is your life simply about indulgences these days?"

Brie tried to figure out how she'd arrived at the diner, and within seconds felt like she'd somehow taken advantage of Carter's vulnerable state by noticing he'd kept his good looks. "Can I see a menu?"

The door to the diner opened and in walked Em. It had been several hours since they'd seen each other, and Brie hoped her aunt had used the time to reflect on all the ways she'd done her wrong, but Em had that cat-that-ate-the-canary look about her.

Em air-kissed Cricket's cheeks. "Patty melt with curly fries and ranch dressing, please."

Brie set the menu aside and held up two fingers. "I'll have the same." As Cricket left, Brie asked, "You still got those fried pickles?"

"Sure do, sweets. I'll bring a batch right over." Cricket pointed. "Watch this one. She's got the hots for the neighbor boy again," she warned Em. "That has trouble written all over it."

Brie gasped. "I do not, and Carter Kessler is not a boy. He's a man."

"Not that she noticed or anything." Cricket laughed all the way to the kitchen.

Brie crossed her arms and leaned back with a huff. "That woman is impossible. She roped me into admitting I thought Carter was cute."

Em sat across from Brie. "I suppose he is if you like the wounded and ruggedly handsome type."

"I don't like Carter Kessler at all. He means nothing to me. He was a childhood infatuation that went wrong—way wrong. I can't believe I ever thought about marrying him. We were twenty years

44

old. What was wrong with you adults? You should have stopped us."

Cricket returned with a pot of coffee, a plate of fried pickles, and a whole pecan pie. Tucked under her arm was a tub of vanilla ice cream she put on the table. "Little miss indicated she was licking some wounds and would need sweets and lots of them."

Aunt Em got bug-eyed, like a cartoon. "You need a gallon of ice cream and a whole pie?"

Cricket poured two mugs of coffee and left the white carafe on the table before leaving. Brie liked the places that did that. It was mighty annoying when you had to chase the wait staff down for a refill.

"You changed my entire life for your selfish needs, and that requires pie." Brie picked up her fork, not bothering to offer any to Em, and dug in, humming as she chewed. By tomorrow she might have diabetes, six new pimples, and be carrying several more pounds, but Cricket's pecan pie was the best in the world.

"Don't stop there. It's better with ice cream." Em yanked off the lid and pushed the container toward her.

Brie nodded and picked up the spoon. She couldn't figure out Cricket. One minute she told her to be reasonable and then she brought her dessert first. She must have seen the mischief on Em's face and knew Brie would need reinforcements. Or she was in on it from the get-go.

With a full mouth and no shame, she said, "What are you up to? I know that look, and it can't be good."

Em sipped her coffee, picked up her fork, and reached over for the daintiest bit of pie, then forked a fried pickle. Any unsuspecting onlooker might think they were pregnant, with that spread before them. "I'm here because you summoned me, and because I feel the tiniest bit of remorse."

Brie nearly choked. "Tiniest. Are you kidding? I uprooted my entire life because you have crow's feet!"

Aunt Em ducked and looked around. "Shh. There might be a soul or two in town that hasn't noticed. Besides, you didn't have a life. You moped around that old house for five years. You're thirty-two going on eighty. Cricket sees more action than you."

Cricket arrived with their patty melts. "I do." She placed the plates on the table and took the bucket of ice cream. "I'll pack this up to go so you can have it later."

"I think I'll need it and a bottle of painkillers. I feel a migraine coming on."

Cricket pointed. "The Five and Dime is in the same location it's always been, right on the corner." Her sneakers squeaked as she spun and walked away.

"Why do they call it a five and dime when nothing in there cost less than a buck?" Brie asked.

Em doused her fries in a lake of ketchup. "I think you can still get penny candy."

Brie rolled her eyes. "That costs ten or twenty cents apiece."

"Inflation, I guess, but let's get back to you and why I embellished the truth." She dragged a fry through the mass murder scene on her plate and set it aside. "You and I are the only family we have left, and Willow Bay is where our roots are. The resort isn't just a building. It's a treasure trove of memories." Brie winced, and Em reached across to hold her hand. "There are good memories and bad but running away doesn't change anything. Isn't it time you came home and restored yourself?"

Deep down, she knew her aunt was right. "Shouldn't the choice have been mine?"

"Honey, you weren't making any choices. Even your anniversary dinner was the same. Cordon bleu with white wine and fingerling potatoes. I bet you steamed the broccolini, drizzled it with butter, and sprinkled it with that pink salt you love. Tell me I'm wrong."

Brie hated that her aunt knew her so well. "I wasn't ready to face Carter."

"I swear I didn't kill Cyrus. He up and died on his own. That man was a hermit for years and ran that resort into the ground. He didn't even open last year. I rarely saw him out and about. Then a few weeks ago, there was an ambulance, and that was it. I did not know Carter was coming back, and I don't think he plans to stay. He's not from here anymore. There's no one here to make him stay."

Brie hadn't considered that he had a life somewhere else, and the thought produced a lump in her throat that hurt to swallow. "Is he married? Does he have a family?" She couldn't imagine someone as good-looking as him not being taken. She tried hard to remember if he'd had a ring on his finger, but she couldn't focus on anything but the way the sunlight had sparkled on the stray grays in his hair.

"I only spoke with him briefly."

"You spoke to him?" Brie leaned in. She hated that she was interested in anything to do with Carter, but she couldn't help herself. "What in the world about?"

"Don't get yourself in a huff over this, but with the Centennial Celebration and Harbor Hop, we are fully booked, and I'm getting more calls than I can handle."

Brie narrowed her eyes. "What are you up to?"

"I subleased The Kessler, and I thought you could help with it for the summer. I also might have told Carter you might be interested in purchasing it."

"You what?"

"Hear me out. It was always part of the plan to own the entire beach complex, and now that you've sold your home and need to reinvest, it seems wise to consider putting it in the property next door. After it's up and running, the revenue would pay the mortgage. You spent your entire marriage to David refurbishing that old house in Louisiana, so you have the skills to make the resort shine. Seriously, you could take that piece of coal and turn it into a diamond. And if I'm allowed to be a little selfish when it comes to competition, I wouldn't mind keeping it in the family."

"A little selfish!" Brie picked up her sandwich and took a bite. She was seeing red, and it wasn't the puddle of ketchup on her aunt's plate. "Let me get this straight. No cancer. My ex is back. You've subleased his resort. I'm running it. You've already reinvested my capital gains from the house into purchasing it. Anything else I should know?"

"There are lots of things you should know, but only one that I'm going to tell you. Carter left you that night twelve years ago because he loved you, and he thought he was doing the right thing. He was an idiot, but I'm fairly certain he still loves you, and he'll never make that mistake again. Not many people get a second chance, but you have one." She wrapped her patty melt in a napkin and shoved it into her purse. "I've got a lot to do before tomorrow. By the way, can you start at eight?" She rose. "I love you, Brie, and I'm glad you're home. As for Carter, you like him, or you don't. You work with him, or you don't. He's not necessarily part of the equation. Make it what you want." She left.

As if on cue, Cricket showed up. "That was fast."

Brie took a deep breath. "Can I have that bucket of ice cream back?"

EIGHT

Working with Em was like being run over by a freight train. Carter walked out of his father's lodging the following day to find a honey-do list twenty lines long taped to his door, but Em's list would have to wait because the bay was calling him. There was no point living on the water if you didn't take advantage of an early morning swim. Back in the day, he and Brie would race to the buoy in the inlet every day before breakfast, and when they got back, they always had Tilly's muffins and chicory coffee for breakfast.

He flung a towel over his shoulder and followed the path to the dock. It wasn't in great shape, but he was pretty confident no one would lose life or limb walking on it. He'd spend the next week replacing the boards with dry rot to make sure whatever equity his family had built didn't go away in a lawsuit.

The sun wasn't up yet; only a hint of orange showing on the horizon announced the new day. The water had barely a ripple of a wave breaking its surface. He loved how the reef protected this part of the coastline. It was like a mother hugging a child.

Catching sight of the bobbing buoy in the inlet, he dove from the edge of the pier.

The water was warm, very different from the Atlantic Ocean near his mother's Miami home. As he swam to the buoy, he thought about the distance he'd traveled over the years. He'd always stayed close to a coast, moving from the west to the east, settling near his mother, where he'd worked for his stepfather as a carpenter the last several years. The water was always nearby, no matter where he was. Sometimes he thought he had saltwater in his veins. The eighty-degree Gulf of Mexico was so much nicer than Maine or Alaska's frigid waters.

Each stroke that got him closer to the buoy released some of the tension he felt about being back home. When he left, he thought he'd lost everything he'd ever loved. Now that he was back, he wasn't so sure. It couldn't be a mere coincidence that Brie was here, too. Maybe it was a dream. She obviously hated him, but his mother used to say only a thin line separated love and hate. He just had to cross it.

Out of the corner of his eye, he caught sight of another swimmer breaking water nearby, only they were on their way back to shore, while he was just beginning his swim. Their head came up, and their eyes met for a split second. Brie turned away quickly and kept swimming. He continued toward the buoy, rounded it, and swam back to the dock.

When he pulled himself up, he came face-to-face with a muffin and a to-go cup of chicory coffee with the Brown logo on the front. He looked around to see who'd left it, but no one was in sight. He hoped it was Brie, but something told him his list leaver and breakfast bringer were the same.

He dried off and wrapped the towel around his neck as he walked home. It was funny to think of his parents' home as his, but it was for the time being. With the muffin in one hand and coffee in the other, he took in everything around him, from the sand that gathered between his toes to the guests next door who were already scoping out the perfect lounger and umbrella.

Seagulls picked the shore clean of whatever had been left behind and hadn't been raked up the night before. He made a note to thank Em for keeping his part of the shoreline clean. Apparently, his father had been derelict in his duties, not only to the resort but also to the community.

Whether Carter stayed or went, he'd have to correct the mistakes that had been made, and there were many. As he turned the corner to his private residence, he got another surprise. Brie was sitting on the porch swing, drinking a twin cup of coffee. She wore a floral dress and flip-flops, and her hair was still damp and hung over her shoulders. For a second, she could have been the Brie from a dozen years ago. Even though she was here, her easy smile was gone, and the light in her eyes had dimmed from the hardships of life.

"Brie."

After jumping to her feet, she tugged at her dress as if trying to make it longer, but he liked the way it barely skimmed the tops of her knees. There'd been no denying it then, and nothing had changed—Brie had mighty fine legs. "After eating an entire pie, along with a gallon of ice cream, I realized I may have forgotten my manners. Mama taught me better than that, and I could hear her hollering in my ear all night, 'Private problems don't give you an excuse for bad manners.'"

"You're fine, Brie."

Her sigh sounded like the air being let out of one of those inflatable ducks the kids used in the shallows. A kind of hiss mixed with a squeak. "I'm sorry about your father. I should have sent regards."

He pointed to the swing. "Sit." She stared at it, and he could see the fight within her. He moved to the rail across from the swing, putting distance between them. "I'm sorry to hear about your parents. Losing both is a tragedy."

"My father went first." Her shoulders rolled forward. "It was probably a blessing because I don't think he could have lived without my mom or my mom without my father. I mean, how do you live without half your soul?"

Until that moment, Carter wasn't sure he'd done the right thing. He'd always wondered if Brie could have accepted the truth but watching her swoon over the lie she had believed about her parents confirmed it for him. "How indeed?" The love she thought her parents had was etched on her face.

Had she had that kind of love for her husband? He didn't fault her for falling in love and marrying another man. He'd pushed her away, but now she was back. Where was her heart? The even bigger question was where was his?

He moved off the rail. "Was there anything else?"

Brie's tell when she was nervous or stressed was chewing on the right side of her upper lip until it swelled to twice its size. Right now, it looked like it'd been stung several times.

"There is. I'll be working in your resort as a favor to my aunt, but I don't want to." She looked both ways and then at the ground before raising her eyes to his. "What I'm trying to say is we aren't friends, Carter, and though my aunt may have hinted at me buying your resort, I'm not interested in owning The Kessler. She tricked me into coming to Willow Bay, and I'm not sure I'm staying."

Was it possible for a heart to stop beating and still be able to breathe? He knew they weren't friends, but he'd hoped he could change her mind. Leaving all those years ago, there'd been no closure, and there was no second-guessing where any of this was going, but clearly, they weren't on the same page.

"Thank you for clearing it up, but I'd like to say something to you. I left you for reasons you won't understand, so I won't even try to explain. But there's one thing you should know: I've never stopped loving you, not for a single second." He leaned forward and thumbed up her chin. "I've missed everything about you, from your crooked second toe to the birthmark on your knee that looks like a horseshoe, to the freckle under your right breast that's shaped like a crescent moon." She gasped. "Yes, I remember it all." He ran his thumb over her swollen lip. "Even the way your kisses taste. You may be done with me, Brie, but I will never be done with you." He straightened, smiled, and slowly licked his thumb. "You still wear that grape-flavored lip balm I love." Color rose from her chest to her cheeks.

He went inside and stood there, waiting. After half a minute, she stomped her feet and let out a screech that would scare away any critter within a mile. He grinned. He knew how to get under Brie's skin. He was out of practice, but he sure was going to enjoy getting his mojo back.

NINE

Feeling a headache coming on, Brie marched into The Brown, past her aunt, and straight to the first-aid kit behind the front desk. She opened the box and found it empty. "Where are the extra-strength pain relievers?"

"Headache or some other pain?" Em reached into a drawer but withdrew, empty-handed.

"I feel a migraine coming on from a pain in my ass." She couldn't believe Carter. "That man has some nerve."

Aunt Em smiled. "Do you mean Carter?"

Brie lifted her hands into the air. "Who else?"

Em laughed. "We're out of ibuprofen. Be a darling and run into town and pick some up."

"I thought we were starting today."

Leaning against the counter, Em shook her head. "We can't work if you have a headache. You're not very nice when you don't feel well."

Brie's shoulders sagged. "I'm nice. Why would you say that?"

"Look at you, stomping in here and complaining about Carter

when all he's done is be here. He even generously let us take over his resort. Do you think his father would have been so considerate?"

"Maybe. Did you ever ask him?"

"No way. He only had ears for your mother. Cyrus Kessler wanted nothing to do with the other Browns."

Brie remembered him as a jovial man, but maybe that was all he'd let her see. "He was nice to me."

"You are your mother's daughter." Em reached into the petty cash box and handed her two twenties. "Pick up extra Band-Aids too and stop in at Cricket's and buy another bottle of her honey. Tilly has been using it for eye cream. She heard it helped with crow's feet, but nothing works for that except good genes, Botox, and filler. I won't be the one to burst her bubble. She finally stopped talking about leaving, and I want to stay on her good side." Em winked.

"She wasn't ever going to leave. Tilly wants what we all want —to belong to something bigger and feel necessary. It's important to feel needed and wanted."

Em kissed Brie on the cheek. "Now you know why I wanted you home." A guest came inside and went to the counter to talk to Em about renting a rowboat.

Brie headed back to her bungalow to get her keys. Everywhere she looked, she saw her mother's special touch, like the seashell and sea-glass collection in a jar on the table. The sand dollars framed on the wall. Olivia Barrett Brown had been creative, and all these little treasures were her gifts to the guests.

On her way to the car, she glanced at The Kessler and found it sad and empty looking. Was that how Carter saw it, too? He'd left a thriving business and returned to a place as dead as a mortuary. She looked for him, but his truck was gone.

Maybe that was why Aunt Em wanted to use the space. It

wasn't that she needed the money. She saw how devastatingly abandoned the place looked. It was hard on Carter, the people who used to work there, and hard for Em, since it reflected poorly on The Brown Resort to have a vacant and unkempt property next door.

She drove into town. Parking was at a premium, and she had to drive up and down Main Street twice before a car pulled out, leaving a space in front of the Five and Dime.

"Perfect." Brie loved it when a plan came together, and since this was her first stop, she took it as a good omen for the rest of her day.

She went inside, made a beeline to the pain meds, chose the industrial-sized bottle, and did the same for Band-Aids. The cashier at the counter seemed familiar, but Brie couldn't place her. A lot had changed in the time she'd been gone, and yet everything felt the same. Willow Bay would always be the home in her heart.

"I heard you were back." The cashier rang up her items.

Brie looked at her name tag. "Haisley?" The only Haisley she'd known was a girl two grades behind her in school, but back then, she'd had buck teeth and bad hair. This woman was beautiful. "Haisley Harper?"

"That's me." She made change for the twenty. Someone joined her behind the counter. "I'm sorry, but I have to run," Haisley said. "I've got an early lunch thing, but I'd love to catch up."

"Sure, I'd love that. If you want to chat sometime, you can find me at The Brown."

Haisley smiled. "Of course. It's where you belong." She took her purse from under the counter and rushed out the door.

"Did you need anything else?" the replacement cashier asked.

Brie picked up her bag. "I'm good."

She walked out into the sunshine. Looking down Main Street, she took in all the businesses that had come and gone in the time she'd been away. The tailor was gone, and in its place was a dry cleaner. Farther down was the candy store, and she wondered if Tiffany was in. When she got there and glanced inside, Tiff wasn't there.

The bank was at the corner, with the sheriff's office directly across. Brie had always thought that was smart city planning. On the other side of the sheriff's office was a gift store, but it used to be a shoe shop. She imagined overnight shipping and shopping malls put it out of business. Next to that was a candle shop and then the florist.

She poked her head in and waved to Trudy, who looked at her like she didn't know who she was. "It's Brie."

"Why, of course. Welcome home, honey. It's good to see you."

"It's good to be back." That felt more like the truth than a lie. "I'll see you around." In front of Cricket's diner, her tummy rumbled. She was only supposed to get honey, but her body was begging for more.

The door opened, and one of the local firefighters appeared. "Ma'am." He held the door for her, and she entered.

Had she arrived at the ma'am stage of her life? For the last five years, she'd been wallowing in sorrow and self-pity while her youthfulness packed a bag and left. "Thank you." Inside, she breathed in happiness, which today was the smell of bacon and maple syrup.

"I knew you wouldn't be able to stay away," Cricket said as she approached. It was halfway between breakfast and lunch, so the diner wasn't packed, but it was still hopping. "I have key lime cream pie and spiced butternut squash pie, but I'm low on ice cream, so if this is a 'feed your sorrow' trip, you'll have to make do."

Brie sat at a table along one side, since all the booths were taken. Across the diner, Haisley was sitting alone, anxiously tapping her fingers on the table.

"This is a 'feed my stomach' trip, and Aunt Em wants more honey."

"I'll have to have a talk with my bees and see if they can up production."

"You make your own honey?"

Cricket laughed so hard, she snorted. "I have skills you've never seen before, but the day I can make honey, I'll no longer be called Cricket. Everyone will refer to me as Queen Bee."

"You are the queen bee."

"You don't have to butter me up. I already told you I'm short on ice cream."

"I'll have bacon and pancakes."

"You want coffee?"

Brie shook her head. "I've had my quota, but I'll take a water, please."

Cricket walked away, and Brie stared at Haisley, who looked as nervous as a hen in a foxhole. The front door opened, drawing her attention, and Carter came in. He glanced around, and his eyes met hers. He gave her a slight smile and nod, and she was certain he was going to come over. Part of her wanted him to. She wasn't sure if she was in the loathe him or like him camp, but he felt like home. Was it possible to hate someone and still want them around?

She pointed to the chair, but his attention went to Haisley, whose nervous demeanor was replaced with a broad smile. Was Carter her early lunch thing?

Jealousy like she'd never felt before surged through her. Less than an hour before, he'd been licking her lip gloss off his thumb, and now he was dining with a beautiful woman two years younger than her and four years younger than him. She vibrated with anger.

Cricket returned with the water. "Drink this. You look like you're ready to combust."

She picked up the glass and downed it, but it did nothing to cool off her temper. "He was confessing his love to me a little while ago, and now he's sitting with her."

Cricket leaned over and whispered, "Did you tell him you loved him back?"

"What? No. I don't love him."

"You feel something for him, or you wouldn't be so darn angry he's eating with another woman. I'll be back with your breakfast."

Carter and Haisley talked and smiled over a cup of coffee and a piece of pie. She bubbled and boiled inside as the two of them had an enjoyable time.

Cricket set her plate on the table. "You need anything else?"

Brie frowned. "I may need pie after all."

"For a woman who says she doesn't care, you sure do a lot of emotional eating. Maybe it's time to be honest with yourself. A part of you never stopped loving that boy."

"Not true. I loathe him."

"Loathe and love are second cousins."

Left to her pancakes, bacon, and a side of misery, Brie hated to admit it, but Cricket was right. A part of her still loved Carter, but she'd take that to the grave. She gobbled her breakfast and couldn't stop staring. Not once did Carter's attention leave Haisley.

Cricket brought her the honey and the bill. After Brie paid it, she rose and started for the door, but her darned feet had a mind of their own, and she found herself standing in front of Carter and Haisley. She looked at him first and then turned to her. "Was this your lunch thing? A date with my—"

"Your what?" he asked. "Boyfriend? Fiancé? You made it perfectly clear you wanted nothing to do with me this morning."

Brie's face was so hot, she feared it might blister from anger. "It didn't take you long to move on. Seems like some things never change." She gave the woman a fake smile. "He likes grape lip gloss. I bet you get a discount on it where you work. I'd stock up." She turned to stalk off, but he grabbed her arm.

"Not that I owe you an explanation, but Haisley is interviewing for the front desk job at The Kessler. Your aunt set up the meeting."

"Oh." She wished the floor would swallow her. "I just thought—"

Haisley cleared her throat and stood. "I don't need any drama in my life. I have enough. You guys have more issues than *Better Homes and Gardens*." She gathered her things. "I think I'll stay where I am. At least at the Five and Dime, there aren't any exes looking like they want to shank me." She left in a hurry.

"You're acting like a jealous girlfriend. Funny coming from someone who doesn't even want to be friends." He glared at her. "What are you playing at, Brie?"

As hard as she thought about it, she honestly didn't know.

TEN

Carter's head spun. Just that morning Brie told him she wanted nothing to do with him, and now she was standing in front of him with a scowl on her face, looking like she was weaned on a pickle. She suddenly went from red-faced to pale. "Are you going to be sick?"

"I'm sorry. I let my emotions get the best of me."

His heart swelled. If her emotions were anger and jealousy, then she still had feelings for him. "You want to have a seat?" He pointed to the bench seat across from him.

She shook her head but sat anyway. She appeared to be at war with herself, and while it shouldn't have given him any pleasure, he was glad her feelings for him weren't as cut and dried as she wanted him to believe.

Cricket rushed over with another glass of water. "You need that pie now, or will this do it?"

"Water is fine."

Cricket stared at Brie. "Yeah, right. Key lime or squash?"

With a weak smile, Brie ordered the key lime.

"It's good." Carter pointed to his empty plate. "Cricket always has the best pie in the state."

"Don't tell Tilly that, or she'll spit in your dinner the next time you dine at The Brown."

He reared back. "Would she?"

"No, but she'd tell everyone she did. Tilly talks a big game, but she's really a softie."

He picked up his coffee and drank. "That seems to run in your circles. You talk a big game, too, Brie."

"What do you mean?" She lifted her water and gulped it.

The Brie he knew didn't have a jealous streak, but he'd never given her a reason to be jealous. She'd never seen him with another woman. While he was disappointed Haisley was no longer interested in the position, he was happy it all went down the way it had. It gave him hope there was still a chance for Brie and him. "You're jealous."

Cricket dropped off the pie and jumped into the conversation. "Smart boy. You'd be wise not to entertain other women until you figure out where you stand with this one." She turned to Brie. "You need to be honest with yourself." Cricket was gone before they could respond. Silence stretched between them like a concrete wall.

Brie finally cleared her throat. "I will admit to being thrown for a second."

Carter chuckled. "A second? You sat over there like an inferno."

"How would you know? You didn't even look at me. You only had eyes for Haisley." She picked up her glass and popped a few ice cubes in her mouth.

"I saw you. And even if I hadn't, I felt you. You threw flaming eye daggers at me." He rubbed his arms and chest. "A few were direct hits."

"If I'd thrown anything at you, they would all have been bull's-eyes. I have excellent aim."

"You were angry because I was with another woman."

"Are you with her?"

Carter was enjoying this conversation because possessive Brie was coming back, and he loved that she cared. "Don't be ridiculous. Have you already forgotten I wasn't on a date? It was an interview—which you ruined, by the way. She was the perfect candidate."

"What makes her perfect? Is it because she's pretty?"

Did she realize how ridiculous she sounded? "No, Brie, because she's qualified. She's been the assistant manager at the Five and Dime for years. She knows how to keep books, answer phones, and offer excellent customer service."

Brie took a bite of her pie and sank lower in the booth. "Couldn't you hire someone that wasn't so perky and cute?"

"I'll keep that in mind the next time someone applies for the job."

"I thought I had that position?"

"So did I until you made it clear you wanted nothing to do with me or the resort."

She nodded. "Look, you and I aren't a thing."

"There you go again." He wanted to laugh, but he didn't. He couldn't force Brie to see what was still there. "Okay, I'll respect your decision."

She took another bite of pie. After she swallowed, she said, "There's a saying about never crossing the same bridge twice."

"That's probably right unless what you want is on the other side."

"All I see is heartache and pain. Haven't we experienced enough of that for a lifetime?"

He reached over and covered her hand. "I can never say I'm sorry enough."

She pulled money from her purse and set it next to her half-eaten pie. "What you did to me was unforgivable." She rose and left.

Cricket quickly came and took Brie's place. "That girl still loves you."

"I don't know, Cricket. She feels something, and I'd like to believe it's love, but I'm not sure."

"It creams my corn that you two can't figure it out."

"It's complicated."

"You want to talk about it?"

"I don't have time, but I'll be back another day so we can chew the fat."

She swiped the dishes from the table. "First pie is on me." She picked up Brie's money. "That girl has had lots of pie since she got to town. That should tell you something."

"Sweet tooth."

Cricket bopped him on the head with the bottom of a plate. "I've known you since you were wet behind the ears, and there's nothing you can't have if you put your mind to it."

He was a go-getter and had never failed at anything except Brie. "She may be right. That bridge might not be sturdy enough for a second crossing."

"Don't be stupid. Shore it up before you take a chance." She pivoted and walked away.

Since he didn't pay for his pie, he left her a hefty tip. Cricket was more than a restaurant owner. She was like Yoda and the Golden Girls mixed into one. She always seemed to have what a person needed when they needed it.

Her advice had hit home. He needed to shore up that bridge, but how? Something told him to lie low for a while. They said absence made the heart grow fonder, and he hoped a little time and space would do that for Brie. She'd loved him once. Was it possible for her to love him again?

ELEVEN

It had been three days since Carter told her he still loved her. Three days since she'd run into him at the diner. Three days since she'd realized she had unresolved feelings.

"Can you get the towels?" Em asked.

They'd finished lunch and returned to The Kessler. The staff had stacked linen in piles on tables in the hallway, and she had to give everyone credit. On day one, she hadn't thought it possible the place could open in a week, but with a lot of elbow grease, and Em cracking the whip, everything was coming together.

Carter had also been burning the midnight oil, which might have explained his disappearing act and not that he was avoiding Brie.

"Where are you hiding Carter?" Brie looked around as if expecting him to jump out.

Em took the master key to the rooms and led the way. "I'm not hiding him. He's a busy man." She pointed to the floors and ceilings. "These don't get clean by themselves, and we have a tight schedule and budget. We also have a skeleton crew, but Carter is taking care of that. He found his father's old payroll and coaxed some of the staff into returning. They'll arrive on Friday before the guests. You'll be happy to know we won't need you as much as originally planned."

Brie sucked in air like she'd been gut-punched. "What do you mean, you don't need me? The Haisley interview was a bust. I thought you wanted me to manage things?"

"You've made your position quite clear to both of us. You're unhappy about being summoned back to Willow Bay. The way I got you here was underhanded, but I don't regret you being here. It's good to have you home." She opened the door to room 102. The bed had been stripped and was ready for new linens. Em shook out a sheet and billowed it across the bed with a flip of her wrist. "Carter has been respecting your wishes and giving you space."

"He's been treating me like I have the plague."

Em took the crisp top sheet and spread it out. They worked like a Swiss watch. Em tucked while Brie turned, and they put the room back together in no time and moved on to the next.

"You can't have it both ways. You don't get to push and pull at the man. Either you want him around or you don't. You tell him to stay away, then show up on his doorstep. You act as if you don't care about him and then go into a jealous rage at the diner."

There was no doubt Aunt Em had gotten the lowdown from Cricket, so there was no point in arguing.

"If I didn't know better, I'd think someone hit you over the head recently and gave you brain damage. You're all over the place."

They started on the bed in the next room. "Excuse me for being a little confused. I thought I was coming home to an emaciated aunt with cancer, and what I run into is my old flame, who looks better than he did in high school. Is that fair? I mean, look at me. I put on the freshman ten and the sophomore twenty."

"And lost the widow forty." Em frowned. "You need to eat more. Tilly made you those sticky buns you like."

"Sticky buns are exactly what the name implies. They stick to your buns."

"I'm pretty certain Carter wouldn't mind if your buns were a little sticky."

"Why all the obsession with Carter? He left me high and dry." She tucked a pillow under her chin and shimmied on the case. "He had the audacity to tell me he left for reasons I wouldn't understand, as if I were an idiot. Then he said he wouldn't try to explain."

"Brie, no two people look at life the same. What Carter knows to be true is different from what you know. Maybe he doesn't explain because he realizes you'll never see it the way he did."

They worked in silence, completing the rest of the rooms by the end of the day. As Brie was leaving The Kessler, Carter came in.

He stopped dead center in the entryway. The setting sun backlit him, making him look like some sort of god. He had no right to look so good, and she had no business looking. The feelings Carter was stirring in her made her feel guilty—like she was cheating on David—but she knew that was plain crazy because he was never coming back. Aunt Em was right. She had to move on.

"Thank you for helping, Brie." He glanced past her to Em. "Margot will be here in the morning."

"Margot?" Brie asked. She scrolled through the Rolodex in her mind for all the Margots she'd ever known, only found one, and didn't like it. "Are we talking about Margot Kincaid? The same Margot who was on the cheerleading squad and hemmed her already-short skirt two inches shorter, so you'd see her good China each time she bent over?"

Carter looked at her, expressionless. "Was she on the cheerleading squad? I don't remember. Back then I only had eyes for you. I'll have to ask her when she shows up tomorrow."

"I can't believe you'd hire her. This is a respectable establishment. You're renting rooms by the night, not by the hour."

"Brie!" Em rarely yelled, and her voice echoed off the pineapple chandelier. "You apologize right now. What's gotten into you?"

"It's okay," Carter said with a grin.

She'd seen that smile before. It was his I'm-getting-under-your-skin smirk, and he knew exactly what he was doing. If she didn't know better, she'd think he hired Margot Kincaid on purpose, because if there was one person she didn't want within a hundred miles of Carter Kessler, it was that woman.

"Argh! You were the most impossible boy, and you have grown into an impossible man."

He chuckled. "You're still beautiful." He pulled a piece of paper from his back pocket and handed it to Em. "I got everything on your list finished. If you don't mind, I think I'll take a swim."

"Enjoy the water," Em said. "I'll have Tilly bring you something to eat."

"I'd appreciate that." As he was brushing past Brie, he stopped. "You want to race me to the buoy?"

"You trust me to be in the water with you and not drown you?"

He laughed. "I imagine you want to, but you'll have to catch me first." He moved out the front door like a man on fire. "I'll meet you at the pier in five minutes. Don't be late. I'm not going easy on you."

She ran after him. "You think you can beat me?"

"I could float on my back and beat you." He took off his shirt.

"Have you looked in the mirror lately? You're as thin as a wafer. If you sank, you'd be mistaken for a flounder."

"Have *you* looked at yourself in the mirror lately?" She eyed his broad chest and slim hips.

"What's wrong with me?"

"Not a damn thing, and it pisses me off." She ran to her bungalow, yelling, "I'll beat you to the buoy, Carter Kessler. You'll see." She threw open her door, and it bounced off the wall and nearly coldcocked her, but she sidestepped, and it slammed shut. "Game on, Carter. You are going to regret a lot of things. The first is leaving me twelve years ago. The second is challenging me to swim to the buoy because I'm fierce. Mark my words, you will most definitely regret hiring Margot Kincaid. That girl was once the bane of my existence, and I'll be darned if she's going to be a bee in my bonnet now."

Brie opened a drawer and rummaged through her things to find the teeniest, tiniest bikini she owned. If Carter thought he'd only had eyes for her in high school, let him see her in this.

He was waiting for her on the end of his dock. She strolled toward him, exaggerating the sway of her hips. Was she too thin? Probably, but that didn't stop him from gawking at her and then glaring at the men who followed her with their eyes as she went by.

"This isn't a nudist beach," he said.

"I'm wearing a bathing suit."

"I think you forgot to put it on. What you're wearing is more like floss and Band-Aids." He stood behind her like a wall, blocking anyone's view. "Let's go." He pushed her into the water.

She came up sputtering. "Why would you do that?"

"You looked cold standing here in the nude."

She trod water. "You're jealous."

"About as jealous as you are of Margot." He dove in, and when he broke the surface, he said, "Go."

He was a body length ahead of her before she realized the race had begun. There was little chance of her winning, but she had a feeling her competition with Carter had just started. Was it more important to win the battle or the war, and what was she fighting for?

She chased him to the buoy and back. When she reached the dock, he was there, leaning down and holding out a hand to help her up, lifting her like she weighed nothing. He wrapped her in the towel and a hug.

"Good job." He rubbed his hands over the towel, helping dry her off, as he had all those years ago. She melted into him for a second but caught herself and stepped back. It would be so easy to fall into a time when life was easy, when summer break meant sleeping in until ten, and nights were spent sneaking kisses under the old willow tree.

He stepped aside to reveal a candlelit table. "Just to be clear, I didn't set this up."

Tilly was peeking around the resort's welcome sign. "I can see the culprit. She's about five-foot-five and makes the best apple strudel known to man." She lifted her nose. "And if my senses haven't misled me, I think she's made her famous schnitzel with spätzle."

He pulled out a chair. "Will you have dinner with me? You can hate me again tomorrow."

She sat. "I don't hate you, Carter." *I just can't let myself fall in love with you again.*

TWELVE

T wo weeks ago, Carter was working on a house in Miami, and now he was sitting at the end of a dock, eating dinner by candlelight with his first and only love. He took the silver domes off their plates and set them aside. The steam from the brown gravy rose into the air. "That smells amazing."

She shifted. "You have to remember this dish. Tilly made it every year on Christmas Eve."

He dipped his fork into the gravy and tasted it, and a flood of memories came crashing back. He'd loved dinners with Brie and her family, and when he thought about her family, it was everyone, from the staff to the stray animals she fed out the back door. His family had been more discerning about who they let into their circle. "Does your family still do that Christmas cookie exchange? I swear, there were hundreds of cookies every year coming out of your kitchen."

"Thousands, and I'm not sure. I only came back to Willow Bay once for a visit and twice for funerals." She looked out at the water. The sun was setting, and the orange glow shimmered off the surface. Though they were technically a part of the Gulf of Mexico, they were an inlet and their own little bay. It was an oasis of sorts that had always seemed like a piece of heaven. "Why did you leave?"

He wanted to forget their past tonight. He owed her an answer, but he just wanted to enjoy the moment. "Can we enjoy this evening without harking back to the past? There's a clear sky and look at those stars." Only a few wisps of clouds were around. The warm breeze was gentle and carried the scent of summer flowers mixed with ocean air. It reminded him of happier times. "We have all summer to hash over what happened. Let's stay in the present."

She seemed to think about his request for a moment and then nodded. "Okay." She forked something that looked like a noodle and put it in her mouth. "If you don't remember, that's spätzle, and it's like a noodle but with a dumpling texture."

He tasted the spätzle and then the schnitzel. "This will put a few pounds on me."

"You look good." She smiled.

"You look good too, Brie. I was surprised to see how slim you'd become. But as long as you're happy and healthy, that's all that matters." It was a diplomatic answer. The truth was, she could stand to put on twenty pounds, and if he had his druthers, he'd be happier with thirty, but he'd lost his vote long ago.

"It's been a difficult few years, but you don't want to talk about the past."

"Not true. I don't want to talk about *our* past, but I'd love to hear what you've been up to."

She smiled. "I refurbished a lot of old properties."

"Is that what you went to school for at LSU?"

She laughed. "No, I got my degree in marketing and then went to work for a law firm, but one day this company came in to restore the building, and I was captivated. I paid more attention to what they did than my job. I got fired and was hired by Regal Restoration. From that point on, I restored old houses. Eventually, David and I bought an old house." She looked at her plate. "Sorry, um, David is my—"

"Husband. I know."

"How did you know?"

He wasn't sure how much to tell her, but she needed to know this. "I went looking for you and tracked you down to Louisiana. By the time I found you, I was too late. You were with someone, and there was no way I'd ruin your happiness twice, so I left."

"You were there?"

He nodded. "Yes. I couldn't stay away. Were you happy?"

"He was a good man."

He reached across the table and set his hand on hers. "That's not what I asked you. I asked if you were happy?"

"Yes, we were happy, but he died too soon, and we never got to figure out how happy we could be. Like everyone, we had our issues, but he was good to me, and we were good together. I think he knew a part of me would always belong to you, and for that, I felt guilty."

"Oh." His heart ached, knowing he had caused her extended pain.

She shrugged. "David knew that and felt some of me was better than none of me. When you've been hurt that badly, you hold things back, so if someone hurts you in the future, something remains."

A tear slipped down her cheek. He wanted to pull her into his arms and hold her, but he figured it would only set them back. He'd been honest with her and told her he'd searched for her, and she'd returned that honesty, though it had felt like a razor to his heart. He deserved nothing less. "Tell me about the house."

She slid her hand out from under his to swipe at her cheek. "Beautiful Victorian. It was a real gem." She held out her hands. "I have the calluses to prove how hard I worked on that house. David and I did everything, which is why I'm so angry at Em for lying to me. That house was a labor of love and held many memories."

"So is this place. This is also your legacy. If not for a stupid decision made years ago, you'd still be here. There would have been no David, no calluses, and no Victorian."

"Life is comprised of many small decisions that have great impact. Like David trading shifts that day. He shouldn't have been on that mission in Kandahar, but the guy he traded with wanted to call his little girl for her birthday. I can't fault David for giving a soldier time to spend with his daughter. Can you imagine? If he hadn't traded shifts, that young father would be dead, and that little girl would be without him. Then again, my husband would be alive. It's crazy how one decision can alter so many lives."

She didn't have to tell him that. He'd played that night he found his father and her mother in the boathouse in his head a thousand times, and there was always a loser. "Speaking of children, I thought you'd have some."

"I guess it wasn't in the cards for me. It's not as if we didn't try, but it didn't happen. Maybe it was for the best because I can't imagine being a widow, raising kids alone."

"Do you think you'll stay in Willow Bay?"

"I don't know. I tried to get my house back, but apparently, there's no fourteen-day seller's remorse clause."

"If it's any consolation, I think Em feels bad."

Brie finished chewing and swallowed. "I know she does, but it won't stop me from milking it. I mean, who does that?"

"Someone who loves you. Imagine what people will say about her for doing it. She was willing to face public opinion to get you here."

"We're talking about Aunt Em. She decides public opinion in Willow Bay."

"You're probably right."

"What about you? Did you ever get married?"

He wished he could avoid the subject, but he'd only have the time it took to chew and swallow what he'd just shoved in his mouth to delay answering. He gained a few seconds by sipping water. "Nope. No wife, kids, or pets."

"Sounds lonely."

He didn't want to talk about himself. He wanted to learn about her. Becoming friends again was one way to shore up that bridge. "Did you get that basset hound you always wanted?"

"Nice change of subject, and no, I did not.

"Why not?"

"David didn't like dogs." She moved food around her plate, and he knew the meal was finished, but dessert remained.

"I think we have strudel," he said.

"Tilly's is the best. It's an old family recipe that goes back generations. Speaking of generations, are you going to sell the resort?"

That was a question that had been in his head since returning. Two generations of Kesslers before him had owned this land. To sell it felt like he was pissing on his ancestors' graves, but he didn't feel like he belonged here. He hadn't belonged anywhere after he left. How was it he was a man without a place? "I can't honestly say, but I know I can't sell it in its current condition, and I don't have the skillset I need to get it into shape."

"Sure, you do. I've seen work you've done."

"That's just labor, but it needs a designer's eye, and I can't afford to bring in someone to advise me about colors and window treatments."

She cleared her throat. "Did I not just tell you I'm a professional home restorer?"

"You did, but I can't afford you, and you don't want to work for me."

"True, but what if I was doing an old friend a favor?"

He chuckled. "Darlin', you're giving me whiplash. Weren't you just telling me we weren't friends?"

She seemed to deflate. "I'm sorry. It's been a whirlwind since I got here. Tell you what. Let's start over." She offered her hand. "I'm Brie Watkins, and I specialize in historic home restoration. I can't help but notice your resort is a mess. I'm staying the summer with my Aunt Em and could use a project to keep my mind off things. I'd love to volunteer my time."

He took her hand. "Hello, Brie Watkins." He hated that last name attached to hers, but he'd live with it for now. "My name is Carter Kessler, and my father recently passed away. We were estranged for over a decade, and while I was gone, the place fell apart. I'm skilled with a hammer but haven't got a clue about paint and décor. I accept your offer." He cut the strudel and served her half. "I hear this is the best strudel for miles."

"I'd say it's the best in the state." She took a bite and then another and kept up that pace until she was finished and eyeing his.

"You want mine?"

"Oh, heavens no. I know where to get more. I'd even bet there's a piece on the table in my bungalow."

"Is Tilly still making you those awful no-bake cookies?"

"We have agreed there will be no more no-bake cookies ever made at the resort."

"It's a miracle."

"When I showed up, she had a plate of them, but we had a reckoning, and it's all settled."

"It seems like a lot of things are getting settled." Settled was a good word for what he was feeling. The last dozen years there'd been movement but in no real direction. Now he was back where it had all started. It seemed like the right place to figure everything out. "Sometimes you have to start over."

"Maybe you're right." The breeze kicked up, and she shivered and pulled the damp towel over her shoulders.

"Let's get you back to your bungalow."

She stood. "I know where it is. Besides, I should bring this back to the kitchen." She gathered the plates into a pile.

He stopped her. "I've got it, and I've got you. Don't forget who raised me. You're not the only one who suffered through cotillion classes. I try to always be a gentleman." He offered her his arm like any well-bred southern man would. "I'll take care of this as soon as I deliver you to your door."

They crossed the sand to the cement walk that led her to her bungalow, and at her door, she hesitated. "You know, I wished you'd get a thousand warts at one point."

"Really?"

She laughed. "Yep, and leprosy, but I knew that wasn't nice, so I changed that to a big undergrounder pimple that hurt like hell."

He couldn't help loving her. "I got that one." He pointed to the tip of his nose. "Right there. I swore it was from eating all those Boston Baked Beans, but now I know." He tapped his head. "Note to self. Don't make Brie angry, or she may release the plague on me."

"You've got enough on your plate right now. I don't need to add anything else to it." She opened the door. "Did you really hire Margot Kincaid?"

"I did." He laughed. "Are you jealous?"

THIRTEEN

B rie gazed at Margot Kincaid from behind the door of the screened-in porch. She'd changed over the years, but life hadn't been unkind to her. She still had that sparkly cheerleader personality that shined when guests arrived, as one had a moment ago.

"Stop gawking and open the door," Em said. Her arms were full of towels.

Brie swung the door wide to let her aunt inside but didn't follow. She felt out of place. Today the lobby belonged to Margot, who would stand and greet the guests, as Claudia used to all those years ago.

"Don't plant yourself there like a knot on a log. Come here and help me."

"Me? You've got her." Brie pointed accusingly at Margot as Em grunted and thrust towels at Brie, nearly knocking her over.

Margot finished with the guest and rushed around the desk. "Let me help you." She took half the towels and set them on the back counter. "Thank you for bringing these. Guests are already asking for them." She squinted. "Is that you, Brie? I heard you were back in town."

Carter appeared from a side door and said, "It's all fixed."

"Bless your heart," Margot gushed and squeezed his arm. "I just couldn't get that drawer unstuck to save my life."

Em pointed to the buttons of Margot's blouse that were undone enough to allow her lacy bra to peek over the edge. "Cleavage is a nighttime accessory. Button up, please." She took the remaining towels from Brie and handed them to Carter. "Make sure the staff knows this is a family establishment. We need to keep things G-rated around here." She marched off to the storage room, with Carter behind her.

"Did she just insinuate—"

"She would never," Brie said. "Aunt Em is a lady, through and through." Em had publicly shamed the woman, but with cleavage came responsibility and Margot needed to be held accountable. Margot hadn't changed one bit. Years ago, it was her skirts that were too short, and now her shirts had seemingly shrunk. While her aunt might have yelled at her the day before for being spiteful, Em had seen firsthand what they were dealing with. For all she knew, Margot would wear cheer spankies and a T-shirt tomorrow to get Carter's attention. "Tell me, Margot. What have you been up to all these years?"

"I married and moved to Dallas for a while. I have three kids," she said proudly.

Just like that, she felt awful for being jealous. A married woman with three kids was trying to make ends meet. "Oh, that's so sweet. Who's your husband?"

Margot smiled. "Ex. Do you remember Dawson Robson?"

"Tight-end-in-high-school Dawson?"

"That's the one. Couldn't nab the quarterback, so I had to

settle." She pulled lipstick from between her breasts and slicked it on. "Anyway. I got pregnant my third year of junior college."

"I thought junior college was only two years."

Margot shrugged. "I was on the extended plan. He did the right thing and married me. We lived in Dallas. Dawson was part of the Cowboys franchise."

Brie's eyes widened. "He made the team? That's amazing." She couldn't imagine Dawson making the Cowboys or fathom Margot divorcing him if he was a pro player, but weirder things had happened. After all, she was back in Willow Bay and never saw that coming.

Margot made a *pfft* sound. "Puh-lease. He cleaned the stadium."

"Well, that's honest work. You have three children?"

She nodded. "I'm living with Mama until I can find another man, but I hear Carter is single." She raised a perfectly plucked eyebrow. One thing about southern girls was they were taught from the moment they came out of the womb to take care of themselves, and Margot looked as pretty as a store-bought doll. "You're not after him again, are you?" She leaned in. "I heard he ran from you once. I can't imagine him wanting to go another round."

Brie stepped back when Carter and Em returned. "He's all yours." Brie hitched her thumb at Margot. "This one is hoping you'll make a fine father to her three kids." She smiled at her aunt. "If you don't mind, I'll head into town to visit Tiffany." She pivoted and waltzed away.

"Wait up," Carter said. "Brie, stop!"

She only got a few steps past the porch before he caught up to her. "What?"

"What was that all about?"

"High school all over again."

He chuckled. "You are jealous."

"No, I'm not." She had been then, and she was now. Not that Margot had anything to offer that she didn't. She couldn't put her finger on what was welling inside her, but it might have been an ugly possessive feeling. She imagined how a dog felt when someone tried to steal its bone. Carter wasn't a bone, and he certainly wasn't hers. It was all so stupid and juvenile, and she didn't understand any of it. "If you want to date Margot, be my guest."

Carter looked confused. "Did I say that? The last person I want to date is Margot. She's not my type."

Brie crossed her arms. "You have a type?"

He wrapped an arm around her shoulders and steered her to her bungalow. "I like them soft-hearted, short-tempered, snarky, and stubborn."

"I'm not stubborn."

"You're like a mule." They stood on her porch. "I have to go into town, and I'll give you a ride if you'd like. Maybe we can stop by the hardware store, and you can guide me on paint colors. You said you'd be my restoration expert. You're not backing out, are you?"

"No. I wouldn't leave you in the lurch."

He leaned in. "And I'll never leave again, Brie. I promise. Tell me you want me to stay, and I will—forever."

"When are you leaving?" His confused look was back, so she clarified. "I mean, to go into town?"

"Oh. How about half an hour?"

"I'll be ready."

He kissed her cheek. "Margot means nothing. You, on the other hand ... mean everything."

She went inside and closed the door. This required a conversation, and the only person she could talk to about such things was gone, but she'd talk to him anyway. She pulled David's picture from a box and set him on the table like she used to. Sitting in the closest chair, she unwrapped the strudel Tilly had left her last night. Tilly was predictable, and Brie was grateful. Moments like this required sugar and lots of it.

"Can you believe he's back?" She'd had countless conversations with David about Carter, and he'd always told her a man didn't leave a woman like her without a good reason. "He says he'll never leave me again. What does that even mean?" She could almost hear him telling her he would never have left if he had a choice. "I know you couldn't help it." She told him about Margot Kincaid and her antics in high school. She ate the strudel and decided what to wear. There was no way she was showing up downtown again without putting on her best face. The first time she'd been there, she wasn't feeling her finest. She didn't have an excuse today, and she wouldn't have her mother turning over in her grave from embarrassment because she dared to go out looking like a dirty dishrag.

She pulled a sundress with flowers on it from the closet and paired it with sandals before touching up her makeup and putting her hair in a messy bun. All the while she kept talking to David, and by the time she'd finished the conversation, she knew what her heart had always known—she was still in love with Carter Kessler.

"Don't you smile at me like that." Anyone else would have thought she was crazy, talking to a picture, but that was their thing. David had always been the calm to her storm. It wasn't the same now that he was gone, but it was all she had. She felt actual pain, thinking about saying goodbye to that comfort, to the man who'd picked up her broken pieces and put her back together. She heard him tell her it was time. The memories of their life together would still be some of the happiest she'd ever known, but it was time to make new ones. David wouldn't want her to live like she was the dead one. Kissing his picture for the last time, she thanked him for being such a good man and listener. Without his love, she didn't know where she would be, but because of it, she was stronger than she'd been. Tucking him back into the box, she knew David would always be a part of her life, but she had to move forward. She wasn't sure if that would be with Carter or someone else, but the knock on the door meant her future had arrived.

Carter wore a fresh pair of jeans, a T-shirt tugged tightly across his chest, and a smile. "Are you ready?"

"Yes, I believe I am." He offered his arm, and she took it, and they walked to his truck. "One thing though. Were you going to kiss me on the porch and chickened out?" She would have bet her life on it.

"Nope." He opened the door and helped her inside. "When and if I ever kiss you again, you will see the stars and the moon. Hell, you may see the Almighty Himself." He shut the door, and she was grateful to have the few seconds it took for him to round the truck for her to catch her breath. That man had always had power over her.

She glanced at The Kessler Resort as he got in. "What about browns and creams and a soft turquoise blue? We can make the resort blend seamlessly into the landscape."

"You just tell me what to do, and I'll do it."

She laughed. "You're easy."

"Yes, but I'm not cheap."

"What are you going to do about Margot? That girl is five dollars' worth of ten-cent makeup."

"All she has to do is show up and do her job. She isn't my problem or yours."

"If you say so." She leaned against the door. Carter's profile was still perfect despite the curve in his nose from when he'd broken it during the homecoming football game. He didn't even go to the hospital. Doc Robinson pinched his nose between his fingers and reset it right there on the bench. She'd stopped the bleeding and told him to get back out there and win the game, and he had, with a Hail Mary pass. That was the thing about Carter. He always came through when people were counting on him. That's why him running off made no sense. "Did you really get cold feet?"

He was silent for a few minutes. "I was twenty. I didn't know my rear end from a hole in the ground. If I had, I wouldn't have left." He parked in front of Sweet on You and turned off the truck. "I'll say this once more, and then it's done. I was an idiot. I was scared, and I made a terrible decision. What held me back no longer exists. I don't expect you to understand. Just having you here is more than I could ask for. It's more than I deserve. You should hate me forever, but you won't, because the Brie I know is kind and forgiving. I'm not asking you to fall in love with me again, but I am asking you to open your heart to the possibility. Am I staying in Willow Bay? That's up to you." He leaned forward. "I'd like permission to kiss you."

She'd learned a million moves at Ms. Daisy's Dance School for Girls, but what her heart was doing was something that couldn't be taught. Carter gently pressed his mouth to hers. The softness of his lips was like a welcoming pillow, and she moved closer, seeking the comfort of his touch. She didn't know whose mouth opened first, but the kiss deepened, and right there on Main Street, she tasted a bit of heaven she'd lost long ago.

When he pulled away, she remained a moment longer, eyes closed and smiling.

"Will that do for now?"

She licked her lips. "Mm, for now." She unbuckled her seatbelt and waited. "Carter Kessler, don't tell me you've lost your manners."

He chuckled. "No, ma'am." He jumped from the truck and raced to open her door. "When should I come back to get you?"

She rose on tiptoes and kissed his cheek. "I'll be ready in fifteen minutes. Do you want a few of those strawberry sweets you used to like?"

"Nope. There isn't anything sweeter than that kiss."

"You are such a suck-up. What do you think those sweet words will get you?"

He laughed. "Not a darn thing, sweetheart. You and I both know I'll be jumping through hoops the rest of my life to please you."

"That's probably true. See you in fifteen."

Feeling lighter than she had in years, she entered Sweet on You to the squeal of her old friend, Tiffany.

"Oh my goodness, is that you, Brie? And did I see you kiss Carter Kessler?" The two women hugged and danced in a circle like they were teens. "Sit down and tell me everything."

For the next fourteen minutes, Brie gave Tiffany the shortened story of her life. When Tiffany went behind the counter and packed up sweets, she promised to come to the resort for a visit when she could. "Are you and Carter back together?"

"I haven't figured that out yet, but let me tell you one thing, that man can kiss."

FOURTEEN

I t had been five days since that kiss, and even though Carter
wanted to pull Brie into every corner and suck the breath out
of her every day, he restrained himself. He didn't want to be like
Tilly's strudel—something Brie gobbled up on the first day and
then wanted nothing after that taste. He wanted her to remember
that kiss and crave the next one.

"Do you like the color?" Brie asked.

"I love it." He hadn't initially shared her vision, but he could
see how right she was as they sanded and painted. His mother had
wanted the place to stand out like the gaudy umbrella that embellished a beach cocktail, like a Mai Tai, but Brie saw the resort as the
drink, with rich rum-brown and tan and only a hint of ocean blue
in the background. "But I'm not a fan of you on that ladder."

She climbed a few rungs higher to annoy him. "I painted my
Victorian while David was on his first deployment."

"And he was happy about that?" He couldn't imagine any man
wanting his woman twenty feet high.

"No, but he liked that I saved us a bundle of money. Do you know how much painting costs?"

He laughed. "I do. That's why you're here. What do you say you come down, and I take you to Cricket's for lunch?"

She swiped at her hair, which was pulled up in a ponytail. "I can't go out in public. I look like something that's been chucked out the side of a lawnmower."

"You look amazing." He was on a ladder next to hers as they worked in tandem to paint the trim. They'd made quick work of the siding and planned to get to the accents and details next week. "Have lunch with me."

"You can have lunch with me. Tilly is making paninis. I thought I'd sneak out to the beach for a few minutes and catch some rays and maybe a quick swim. All the craziness starts tomorrow night."

Lunch sounded good, but the chaos of a Parade of Lights and the Harbor Hop did not. "What bathing suit are you wearing?"

She started down the ladder. "What does it matter?"

He followed. "It doesn't. I was just wondering how many men I'll have to beat up on my lunch break for looking at my girl."

"Your girl, huh?" She tucked her paintbrush into the plastic bag she used every day. He put his brush next to hers and followed her to The Brown's kitchen. "Hey, Tills," she called as she went in the side door. "Can I have two of those paninis?" She waved him inside. "You can come in. No one is going to bite."

"Darn." He wiped his boots on the mat and entered. The kitchen was spotless, and while it looked like pure chaos, with half a dozen cooks running around, it was controlled chaos. Everyone had a job, and they were doing it. It was like a finely orchestrated dance, with people weaving in and out of each other's way.

"You two have a lunch date?" Tilly asked.

"I wouldn't call it a date," Brie said. "It's just lunch."

"I'd call it a date," Carter said, lips quirked.

Tilly pulled a basket from a shelf and filled it with ingredients like chips, cookies, drinks, and cutlery. "If you're alone and having a meal, it's a date." A buzzer went off, and she used tongs to remove hot grilled sandwiches from the machine and place them inside bags before putting a plastic-wrapped picnic blanket on top of the basket and handing it to Carter. "End the meal with a kiss, and it's definitely a date. I'll expect a full report later. Now get out of my kitchen. Can't you see I have work to do?" Tilly shooed them away and closed the door.

"Where to?" Carter looked at the beach, which was packed. The only place that seemed to be free was next to the old willow tree, but he didn't want to suggest it because it held so many memories—good and bad.

As if she could read his mind, she sighed. "Can't avoid it forever." She pointed to the only available spot. "Might as well open the wound now."

"Or close it. It's all perspective." There were two types of people in life: the glass-half-empty type or the glass-half-full, and Brie had always been the latter. He hoped he hadn't taken that away from her, too. He opened the basket under the willow, tore the plastic cover off the blanket, and laid it out for their 'date.' "What's a panini?"

Brie sat, picked up a sandwich, and handed him half. "Tilly says it's a new menu item. This one is ham, turkey, salami, and cheese, grilled to gooey perfection."

"An expensive grilled meat and cheese?"

"I guess so. You know me, add melted cheese, and I'm in."

"At least that hasn't changed."

"What's that supposed to mean?"

"All it means is I'm glad I didn't ruin everything good about you."

"What doesn't kill ya makes ya stronger." She took a bite and closed her eyes. He loved to watch her savoring the taste of it. There was pure joy on her face. "What do you think?"

"I'm jealous of the sandwich."

She socked him in the arm. "Just eat it." Her eyes drifted past him to the tree, and she rose to her feet. "Look." She pointed up to where a branch had broken off, but there was a heart carved above it. Inside it was the initial C and what looked like another C, but it was hard to tell because part of it had been scraped off or removed when the branch came down. He had a feeling it had been an O. "I think your parents carved their initials there."

"Maybe."

"What do you mean, maybe?" She ran her fingers over it. "It's right here. Don't you think it's romantic?"

Upon closer inspection, he was sure it had been an O because the circle was partially closed. "Look around. There are lots of initials carved into this tree." There were at least two dozen. He took her hand and led her around to the other side, where they'd carved their initials in the trunk years ago. "Here are ours, and they are the only ones I care about." He leaned in to kiss her but thought better of making a public display of his affection and took her back to the blanket, where he offered her the second half of her sandwich.

"I guess this isn't a date after all," she said.

"Oh, it's a date, but I'm not performing for the masses. Like your aunt said, this is a family establishment, so we need to keep things G-rated. The next time I kiss you, it's going to be R verging on NC-17." It was a warm day, but the goosebumps rose on her skin. He could tell she wanted more of his strudel-like kisses, but they would come when she least expected it.

After they finished lunch, they spent the rest of the day painting. When it was quitting time, he walked her to her bungalow and leaned in. Her lids closed, and he moved to her ear and whispered, "Let me take you out tomorrow."

"What?" Her eyes popped open in surprise.

"I want to take you out. Were you expecting something else?"

"No, why?"

"You just had a look of expectation about you. Like you want to be kissed."

She smacked him on the arm. "Carter Kessler, you're just being mean. I don't know if I want to go on a date with you."

"You do."

She hit him again. "Whatever. I would invite you in, but you'd probably try to kiss me, and I don't want your lips anywhere near mine."

"You're an awful liar. No matter though because I need to prepare for our date."

"Who said I agreed?"

"You will. Goodnight, Brie."

On the way to his place, he noticed the dock, which had been closed for the season, but it didn't mean he couldn't use it for a private party for two. The Festival of Lights parade was the perfect opportunity to pull out all the stops. It would be the last moment of relative peace they'd have that summer. Saturday would kick off the Harbor Hop, which was basically a game of boat poker that started the summer season and got the Centennial Celebration underway. Tomorrow night was the one time they could relax and be themselves. All hell would break loose after that.

The best thing about the boathouse was it opened to the harbor but closed to everything else as long as he cordoned off the area. With a plan he couldn't put into action until daylight, he climbed in his truck and headed into town. He needed a nice dinner for the date and didn't want to ask Tilly, who would have her hands full with resort guests, so he went to the only other person he knew that could pull off a last-minute miracle, and that was Cricket.

Despite the town being packed, he lucked out with front-row parking at the diner. The last time he was in, he hadn't paid attention, but this time he took in the country décor, with its chickens and roosters and eggs decorating shelves and nooks and crannies as he entered. And like any good diner, this one had a jukebox in the corner, belting out music by Johnny Cash that was as old as Cricket.

"You back for more punishment?" A flash of red sneakers and blue ran toward him. "Come give me some sugar." Cricket hugged him long enough for her hands to test the firmness of his biceps. "Yep, you grew up finer than a frog hair split six ways." She looked him over like she was seeing him for the first time. "She was right, you know."

"Who was right?"

"Brie."

"What did she say?"

"That you're a looker."

"She said that?" He was glad Brie was attracted to him. That could only make the date better.

"You here to chitchat or eat?"

"I came for food and a favor."

She pointed to the one open seat at the counter. "Take it before it's gone."

Carter pulled the menu from the holder, but she snatched it from his hand. "You'll be making my life easier if you order the meatloaf and mashed potatoes."

"Yes, ma'am."

Cricket went to the window and yelled, "One special!"

The person next to him bumped him with her shoulder. "Carter Kessler, is that you?"

She looked familiar but not. He tried to place her and couldn't, and then his nose hurt. "Dr. Robinson?"

"Let me see that beak of yours." She pinched the end of his nose like she owned it and turned him this way and that. "Not bad for a sideline fix." She dropped her hand and picked up her tea, no doubt sweet because there wasn't any use drinking anything else when you were in Willow Bay or Cricket's. He remembered a tourist ordered it unsweetened once when he was a teen, and the entire place went silent.

"How are you?"

She smiled. "If I were any peachier, I'd be a cobbler. I'm not looking forward to the weekend. You know as well as I do the Harbor Hop starts one hundred days of stupid, and my summer will be busier than boobs at Mardi Gras."

Carter choked. He'd forgotten how candid the folks here were. They had no problem telling you off but would always follow it with *I'm prayin' for you.*

Cricket slapped a plate of something covered in gravy in front of him and addressed Dr. Robinson. "Don't be setting your eyes on this one. He's Brie's. They screwed it up once. Let's see if we can't help them fix it this time around."

She laughed. "I like mine a little older, a little wiser, and a lot richer." She eyed him. "There is a cure for stupidity. It's called an apology, and it works wonders on women." She pulled several dollar bills from her purse and set them on the counter. "Flowers don't hurt either. Visit the Yellow Vase. Trudy and her daughter Suri run it." She rose and patted him on the back. "You got this, and if she breaks your nose, you know where to find me."

Cricket leaned against the counter. "What's this favor?"

FIFTEEN

"That boy is up to no good." Em sipped her wine on the porch of Brie's bungalow and pointed to the boathouse at The Kessler Resort. The lights were on, and a shadow moved inside to outside from time to time.

Brie recognized Carter by his tall build and broad shoulders. "I know." She was glad they were sitting in the dark, otherwise, her aunt would see the big grin on her face. "It's kind of bittersweet, don't you think?"

Em topped off their glasses from the bottle on the table. "It's been a long time coming. A day I never thought would happen." Her words sounded a little slurred, or maybe it was exhaustion. She'd been working herself to the nubs since she'd come up with the harebrained idea that they should sublease the rooms from Carter. Since coming up with the idea, her aunt had been forcing them together any way she could. She'd been reading far too many Harlequins over the years. Didn't she know the universe always had a plan, and there was no point in meddling? "What do you think he's up to?"

"You said no good, and I'm sure you're right. Can you believe he gave me a toe-curling kiss five days ago and hasn't touched me since?"

"Maybe you're off your game."

"I'm out of practice, but it couldn't have been that bad. It's like riding a bike." Even though Brie was in the rusty category, Carter had said he wanted more. She was tiring of waiting.

"You probably have to climb on a few times before you get the hang of it again. Maybe you can get a few pointers from Margot. I bet that girl is like a female Lance Armstrong." Em was full of sass tonight, or maybe it was too much wine.

"She's not so bad." Brie had run into Margot a few times during the week, and after that first day, she'd been nothing less than professional. She'd even found some shirts that fit. Her attention had shifted from Carter to a cook from The Brown Resort. This didn't make Tilly happy, because Margot was spending all her breaks in the kitchen getting "cooking tips."

"She's not so good either." Em flopped back in her chair. "If your momma had caught her looking at Cyrus, the way she looks at Carter, that girl would have been hogtied, honeyed, and hung out for jerky."

Em must be drunk because she'd gotten the men mixed up. "You mean my daddy."

Em cocked her head, and her mouth dropped open. She gulped the rest of her wine and set the glass down. "Time for me to go to bed." She rose and bent over to kiss Brie on the cheek, picked up the empty bottle and tottered off to her quarters around the back of the resort. Brie followed her. "I feel you lurking behind me," Em said.

"Just making sure you get inside safely."

Once inside, Em waved her over. "I found a box of your mother's things in the attic the other day. She kept some journals I thought you'd like. It's just old recipes and gardening stuff." She pointed to the corner. "Help yourself." Em held on to the handrail while she teetered up to the second floor and disappeared.

Brie looked at the small box on the entry table. Inside were two leather-bound journals. She picked up the box and glanced around the room. This had belonged to her parents, but it no longer felt like home. It didn't smell like her mother's gardenia perfume or her father's pipe tobacco. The old dark wood was now a soft butter yellow, with floral accented wallpaper. What used to look like an old English library now resembled a garden. It was lighter and brighter because of Aunt Em.

Come to think of it, the whole place was more vibrant with her in charge. Brie held onto that thought as memories of growing up here assaulted her. She'd loved it here, loved her parents, loved her life but had forgotten the sadness that had hung over her home then. A sadness she tried never to think about. She assumed it was because her parents worked so hard. Their commitment to the resort and family took everything, but now she wasn't sure. Maybe she'd only seen life through the eyes of a child—through the kaleidoscope of colors a kid saw when she looked around her. A world full of seashells and ice cream cones and stolen kisses by the willow tree. But the real world was bills and heartache and death and disappointment.

But there was also pecan pie, second chances, and a man named Carter, who was up to something in the boathouse.

She turned off the lights and left. When she moved past her bungalow, she dropped off the journals and continued to the Kessler dock. She desperately wanted to know what he was doing. There was no sneaking up on him because the dock creaked under every step she took. When she opened the boathouse door, he said, "You can't come in here."

"Why not?"

"Because I'm up to something."

"That's obvious. If you were trying to be stealthy, you're bad at it."

"I'm trying to do something special."

"Special is just showing up, Carter. That's all you have to do."

"I'm here now, and I'm not going anywhere."

She stepped back and leaned on the dock railing. "Can I ask you something?"

He exited the boathouse and shut the door. "Anything."

"Am I a terrible kisser?"

He moved so fast she could barely catch her breath before his mouth covered hers. The velvety texture of his tongue was so intoxicating that she lost track of everything except the feel and taste of him. He was peppermint and sex appeal, and she couldn't get enough. After wrapping his shirt in her hand, she tugged him toward her, trying to get a little closer. The handrail pushed against her back until it was painful, but she didn't care. All she wanted was to feel again, and at that moment, she felt everything from the loss of him to finding him again. Years of hurt and anger washed away in that kiss until all that was left were two adults finding their way back to one another.

Carter gave her the weight of his body, and she gladly took it, but the rail was less hospitable. One quick snap sent them plunging into the water below. It was the second time she'd been tossed into the water because of Carter, only this time she surfaced laughing. "I swear you'll be the death of me."

He swam over and wrapped his arms around her. "And you are my life, Brie."

They trod water for several minutes, kissing until she was certain they'd heated the bay enough to poach the fish, and then they headed to shore. Carter was as good as his word. That kiss had not been family-friendly, and neither was his pier.

"You should fix the railing before someone gets hurt and sues you," she said as they dragged themselves onto the beach.

"You already own my heart, Brie. You might as well sue me and take the rest."

"I'm not sure I'm ready for that, but I do like your kisses." She was ready for more but how much more? Her heart was all in, but her brain kept reminding her how much love could hurt. She squeezed water from her hair and tried to squeegee her clothes with her palms, but it was no use. "I should head inside."

"I'll walk you back."

She held up a hand. "No need." She looked at his soaking wet clothes. "Wet jeans chafe. There are times for chivalry and times for common sense. Let's play this one smart. Didn't you say we have a date tomorrow?"

"I'm glad you remembered."

She looked at the boathouse and smiled. "It's a special date, am I right?"

"That's the plan."

"Good dates don't start with chafing. I can find my way home. Thanks for the kiss and the swim." She strolled up the beach to the cement walk.

"Brie."

"Yes?"

"I never answered your question."

She knew exactly what question he was referring to. She looked left and right to make sure no one was in earshot. "What's the verdict?"

"I heard angels sing."

She laughed. "Maybe you hit your head when you fell in the water."

"Or I heard angels."

"Yeah, we'll stick with that."

Despite being weighed down with water, she felt light. She passed bungalow six and counted back to her room. Over the years guests had left their mark by carving initials or symbols, like hearts or stars into the siding. Her father had wanted to sand them all off, but Mom insisted he leave them. She'd said they were legacies of love, and people would come back year after year and remember where their first kiss took place. As she went past bungalow five, a heart caught her attention. It was simple and perfect, and inside was a C and an O. She smiled at all the people who had fallen in love in Willow Bay and wondered where were the mysterious C and O now?

SIXTEEN

Carter woke early despite getting to bed late. It was probably the excitement of having an actual date with Brie.

He laughed at her antics the night before. She hadn't agreed to the date, but she didn't flat out say no either. She acknowledged that it was planned, so he would proceed as if it were a go. The Brie he knew would claim she required little fuss, and that was true, but that didn't mean she wouldn't appreciate the effort.

He started a pot of coffee in the kitchen. His father still had one of those old percolators straight from the fifties, with the metal basket you poured the grounds into. After he set it up and plugged it in, he called his mother.

"Carter Roland Kessler, where have you been?" His mother only used his full name when she was angry. "I've left several messages. I even called the front desk, and some annoying little bird named Margot put me on hold. That's not the Margot you went to high school with, is it? If so, gird your loins."

He sat at the kitchen table and readied himself for what would be a long, one-sided conversation. One thing about southern mamas, or maybe it was only his mother, was that she didn't have a mute button, and once she got started, she went on forever. He listened to her tell him about what a terrible son he was for not checking in, and then she went through his entire birth process to make sure he knew the sacrifices she'd made to bring him into the world. "I'm your mother, and I deserve better."

"Yes, ma'am. I love you, Mama." The coffee was finished, and he poured a cup and doctored it with cream and sugar. He thought about popping two frozen waffles into the toaster, but he'd be at Cricket's shortly, and she'd feed him eggs and bacon and cheesy grits. "Guess who's back in town?" He gave her the shortened version. "I've got a date with her tonight."

"Oh, honey. Do you think that's wise?"

He leaned against the counter, a little dizzy from the slap his mom had just given him. All these years she'd been calling him an idiot, and she was asking him if he was being wise? "Isn't that what you wanted? I always thought you'd be happy to see Brie and me together."

"Well, of course, I would. I always thought you two belonged together. But I don't want to see you hurt again. Those Browns have a way of hurting you."

"You, too." He couldn't forget what his mother must have gone through being married to his father but feeling like the other woman. Then again, he had to consider what his father and Olivia went through. According to Em, they'd been madly in love and forbidden to see each other because of a family feud between their parents. His grandfather and Brie's grandfather came from a generation who believed *he who died with the most toys won.* They were buried on opposite sides of Willow Bay Cemetery, and neither had taken a thing with them, so all the arguing and fighting did nothing for them except perpetuate misery. They'd made sure their only children didn't marry who they loved. They married who was acceptable and ruined four lives, six if he counted his and Brie's, but he was trying to rectify that.

"I'm happy, and it would make me happy to see you happy."

He chuckled. "That's a helluva lot of happy."

"How are things at the resort?"

Did he tell her the truth? That his father had let it go to hell after Olivia passed away? "It needs some work, but Brie has been a lot of help, and Em lent me some staff."

"Lent you some staff? What happened to our staff?"

"I don't know what happened to The Kessler, but it fell apart. I'm putting it back together, though." They both knew what had happened. His mother was well aware the Browns had died. She'd moved to Florida, but gossip traveled via telephone, email, and Cricket's Christmas cards that spilled the beans on everyone in town. If you wanted to know anything about anyone in a town, visit the diner, beauty shop, or doctor's office. Old Mabel Bixby faked an episode of gout every Monday morning to get the weekend news. The only reason Carter knew that was because Dr. Robinson had made him drop her off on his way to school as payment for fixing his nose.

"Are you staying there? You know, nothing good ever happened in Willow Bay."

"That's not true. I happened here, and I'm the best thing in your life."

"Until Frank."

"Is he paying you to say that?"

She giggled and then there was a commotion. "Give me the phone back," his mother said, laughing.

"Hey, son, are you doing okay?" Frank asked. When Frank called him son, he meant it. From the day Carter entered his life, he didn't have to earn his place. He had one.

"I'm good."

"Are you coming home?"

"You know me. Home is where I toss my boots, and right now it's Willow Bay." In the background, his mom said Brie's name.

"Ahh," said Frank. "You got a special date, I hear. Did you get her flowers? What about candy? Girls like candy." Carter made a mental note to stop by Sweet on You. "You fixin' dinner or buyin' it? Honestly, Carter, I've eaten what you cooked, so I'd pony up and buy the girl some food."

"Cricket's making me something special."

"What's a cricket? Around here, that's something you smash under your heel."

"Around here it's a national treasure that makes the best fried chicken, biscuits, and pecan pie you can find, and I mean no disrespect to my mama. Cricket's got me hooked up. The Yellow Vase is getting the flowers ready, and I'll pick up the candy. What else do I need?"

Frank was a robust Italian man with a laugh that could be heard into next week. "I'd say a box of condoms, but your mother would love to be a grandmother, so you might as well skip that step." There was a clatter. "Ouch."

"Don't you listen to him. Brie is a good girl, and good girls don't do things like that on first dates."

"Mama, don't forget Brie and I were a breath away from being married. We've already—"

She talked over him. "I don't want to know."

"She's a widow, Mom. We aren't thirty-something virgins."

"In my book, if you haven't done it in a certain length of time, then you revert."

"What defines that time? I may be a virgin again," Frank said, and a second later, he said, "Ouch."

"All I'm saying is I raised you to be a gentleman," she said. "And I expect you to behave like one."

"I'm pulling out all the stops." He drank his coffee and placed the cup in the old, stained sink. "Which reminds me, I have a few more things on my to-do list, so I'll talk to you later." He hung up before she could argue with him. He hadn't waited twelve years for this moment only to ruin it by rushing things. Their relationship was like a fine wine. He'd pop the cork and let it breathe. They could sip and taste, but it was up to her how much she wanted to indulge.

With so much to do, and time running out, he dressed and went outside. The beach was already full of vacationers, holding their spot for the day and evening. But someone caught his eye. Brie was under the willow tree, running her fingers over the bark. She was wearing shorts and a tank top and took his breath away. He was grateful she wasn't wearing her floss and Band-Aid bikini, or he may not have been able to tear himself away.

FIFTEEN MINUTES LATER, he was at Sweet on You, where Tiffany was standing inside a cardboard box fixed up to look like something you'd see in a Peanuts cartoon. Above it was a sign that read, "Love Advice."

"How much?"

"You don't want advice from me, but you may be the only person in Willow Bay who is unluckier in love."

"Not true. I find love. I just muck it up. So, tell me, sage of love, how do I not mess up this date with Brie?"

She flashed a big ole Texas smile. She must have spent a fortune on those teeth because they hadn't been that straight or white in high school. "You show up this time."

Each time he heard those words, it hurt. It was death by a

zillion cuts because a thousand wasn't enough. "I plan to, and I also plan to bring candy, which is where you come in."

"What about words?"

"What about them?"

"You got any sweet ones? Girls like words."

He scratched his head. "Like poetry?"

She exited the cardboard box and went behind the counter. "Can you sing?"

"Not if she doesn't want her ears to hurt."

"What's your budget?"

"Are we talking candy, or do you have some connection that can get me Garth Brooks? Because I'll go into debt for Brooks, but I have a twenty for candy."

She frowned. "There's no budget when it comes to love."

"There is if you want a second date." She filled a box with chocolates she thought Brie would like. "What about you? Are you dating?"

Tiffany shook her head. "Nope, my life is complicated."

"Whose isn't?"

She rang up the sale, and he left to get the flowers. Walking through town was like a high school reunion and seeing Trudy and her daughter Suri took him back to prom when he'd picked up Brie's corsage. She loved what he thought were odd floral combinations. Waiting for him were a dozen of her favorite flowers, one for each year they had been apart.

His next stop was Cricket's, where the only open seat in the place was under a picture of a rooster that read Nice Cock. He pulled out the menu, then put it back; he'd get what Cricket wanted him to have.

She showed up with a pot of coffee, two cups, and the plate of cheesy grits, bacon, and eggs he'd been craving. Collapsing in the seat across from him, she propped her feet on the bench. "Don't tell the boss I'm slacking, but my feet are killing me."

"You're the boss, and it's only ten-thirty."

"I've been here since five. I bet your lazy little bottom just got up." She poured them both a cup and leaned back.

"Why don't you retire?"

Her feet dropped, and she moved like a snake ready to strike. "The day I retire is the day I die." She held up a finger. "Old man Sanders retired May 5th and died June 6th, Hank Oliver retired April 22nd and died June 6th. Okay, they were together when the house burned down. Despite that, it's bad juju. Wanda Pollard retired in November and was gone by January." She tapped her chin. "She might have moved. I can't remember. Either way, retirement is the devil."

"Got it. No retirement for Cricket." He sipped his coffee.

"This place defines me."

"Nope, you define this place. Without you, it's just a diner. Nothing special. You are Cricket's. I've always wanted to know what your real name is."

"If you tell anyone, I will put something in your food that will give you dysentery for weeks."

He crossed his heart. "Our secret. I was just thinking this town was good at keeping some of them. Why is that?"

She whispered, "Lulubelle. Do I look like a Lulubelle to you? My mother must have been smoking a pipe when she named me Lulubelle Persimmon."

She was right. She didn't look like a Lulubelle or a Lulu. "How'd you get Cricket?"

"Used to collect them as a kid, but don't be telling anyone. I like to be surrounded by mystery."

"I wouldn't consider it."

"Gossip is gossip, and that's different from secrets."

"Educate me." He started eating.

"I plan to." She moved into the corner and kicked her feet out again, getting comfortable. "I love a good tale. Gossip flies all over town. It's when Mae goes to Dolly's to get her hair done, and she thinks she's getting a pleasant brown but comes out with a greenish tint because Dolly forgot her glasses and used ash instead of a warm shade. Now that's gossip. But a secret can be hurtful. A secret is when your father was having an affair with Brie's mother for years. People will talk about Mae's green hair, and it might hurt her or Dolly's reputation, but they'll recover. Dolly will fix it, and the two of them will laugh about it next week. But when it comes to betrayal, well, there's no coming back from that."

"You knew?"

She nodded.

"Who else knows?"

She looked around the diner. "Most people don't see what's right in front of their faces. I knew because both Olivia and Cyrus used to talk to me. When fire burns that hot, you can't douse the flame. It smolders. They lived next door to each other. It was a disaster waiting to happen. The timing was terrible."

"I caught them."

"Did anyone know?"

He shook his head. "I backed out and closed the door."

"The bigger question is why did you leave?"

"To protect Brie."

"You can't protect her forever. She's not twenty anymore."

"I know, but if I'd stayed, I would've had to tell her, and she would have hated me."

"Maybe you weren't protecting her. Maybe you were protecting yourself. You know that saying, 'Don't kill the messenger?' You were afraid to be the messenger."

"Maybe." He hadn't thought of it that way. "I guess I was a coward."

"You were a kid. Now you're a man, and you have a second chance. What will you do?"

"I'll show up."

She eased her way out of the booth. "With my fried chicken and fixin's, and if that doesn't win her heart, you never had a chance to begin with."

SEVENTEEN

The whole town knew she had a date. She wondered if
Carter had put a banner on Main Street or Aunt Em had
called in reinforcements. One minute she was checking out the
carvings lovers had made over the years, and the next she was
sitting in the kitchen of The Brown Resort, being "tended to" by
Charlotte, who slapped something on her face that felt like
hellfire.

"It hurts," Brie complained.

"Oh, stop your fussin'. If it was easy to be pretty, everyone
would be Miss Lone Star State, and we know that isn't happening.
There's only one of us a year."

Charlotte was crowned back in the Stone Age but not on
pageant day. She got it months after, in one of those minor infrac-
tions. The "in case of" printed at the bottom of the contract, which
said you shouldn't pose for a nude magazine. But it didn't matter to
Charlotte how she got it. She wore that crown proudly for the
following nine months, and the next girl had to pry it from her
fingers when her name was called.

Tilly poured chicory coffee and served fruit tarts, while Marybeth caught them up on the town "news." If anyone else had been talking, it was gossip, but since it was Marybeth, she'd add a "bless his soul" or an "I'll pray for her" and call it news.

"Did you see where someone went into our Five and Dime and won the lotto?"

Aunt Em strolled inside and took the end seat. "Millions." She glanced out the window. "It's probably a tourist rather than a local. Too bad it wasn't Carter. He could use some cash flow to get that place in shape."

Tilly dragged a chair over and sat. After a while, Brie's face felt more like it was simmering than boiling.

"Do you think he'll stay?" Marybeth asked.

"He needs a reason to stay." Charlotte whistled. "I'm not a miracle worker. You heard the girl." She wiped off the original goo and applied a second goop that felt cool. "She doesn't even wash her face nightly." Charlotte stuck her face in front of Brie's. "How old did you say your skin was?"

"Two and half centuries."

"Maybe I can get you to look under a hundred. Some men like older women." Charlotte rubbed whatever she'd slathered on until Brie's skin soaked it up. "Didn't your mother tell you the benefits of Nivea or Ponds? Going without moisturizer is like going without coffee or pie. It just isn't done."

Brie would've scowled, but the stuff on her face made it so tight she thought it might crack.

"Oh, and I made you a hair appointment with Dolly at two," Marybeth said.

"What's wrong with my hair?" Instinctively, Brie reached for it, but Charlotte swatted her hand away.

Marybeth's lips thinned. "Nothing, if you're waiting for birds to nest. I've also brought a few things to hide those bones of yours."

"I've been working on that," Tilly said, passing another fruit tart Brie's way.

Marybeth gave her a critical look. "Your ass cheeks are like two communion wafers in a paper sack, sweetie. If no one shook the bag, we wouldn't know they were there." She lifted her purse from the floor and pulled out several dresses. "Camouflage is my color." It was like a magical bag without a bottom. Out came two camo-inspired dresses and a pair of shoes. "I like the green one, but with your blue eyes, the sapphire might be just the trick."

"Definitely the blue," said Em. "And the shoes are perfect."

Marybeth picked up the espadrilles. "You know what they say. The higher the shoe, the lower the morals." They looked at their moderate heels and laughed. "Obviously that was someone who hasn't worn a pair of Jimmy Choos or the latest Michael Kors."

They sat around the table and chatted while Charlotte continued Brie's makeover.

"What do you think Carter was up to at the boathouse last night?" Em asked.

"I tried to sneak a peek, but he wouldn't let me, and then I kissed him again. Boy, can that man kiss. Then the railing broke, and we fell in the water."

Marybeth looked at the ceiling. "Bless this young woman." She turned to Brie. "Your mama isn't here, and your aunt is failing, so I'm going to tell you the best advice I ever got." She cleared her throat. "Men don't buy the cow if you give away the milk for free."

Em laughed. "She wasn't giving him a side of beef, Marybeth. In this day and age, people don't buy anything unless they can take it for a spin first. A woman has a right to take a test drive. Any smart woman would tell you, you don't pick a car until you sit behind the wheel and take it for a spin."

"I'm all about the test drive. Do you know how many lemons I've almost purchased?" Charlotte pulled out what looked like a painter's palette and a box of brushes and went to work on Brie's makeup. "Sometimes all the fun is in the window shopping."

Brie held up her hand. "Hold on, ladies. Don't forget I've taken that one for a test drive and put a deposit on it a long time ago."

Charlotte applied foundation and rubbed it in. "That was an older model. You've got the updated version with upgrades. See what they are before you decide one way or another."

Of the four of them, only Marybeth was married. Brie couldn't remember a time in her life when she'd seen Tilly with a man. The same applied to her aunt. Charlotte dated many. As the town's beauty consultant, realtor, and local busybody, she got around.

"What about you, Em? Where's Mr. Right?"

"Like I told Carter the other day, he must have taken a wrong turn a long time ago and is still lost."

Charlotte waved a brush around. "Your aunt is married to the resort. Unless a man walks inside The Brown and finds her, it isn't happening." She swiped on blush and handed Brie a tube of a new mascara. "Put several coats of that on, and you're done." She stood back and smiled while everyone congratulated her on her masterpiece.

"Put that dress on first," Marybeth said.

Brie took the dress and shoes and went to the bathroom to change. As a kid, she'd spent a lot of time in that kitchen with those women, and it felt like old times, but when she looked in the mirror, she didn't see herself—she saw her mother. It was the first time that had happened.

She checked out the makeup job. It had been ages since she'd paid much attention to her looks. She was raised to put her best self forward, but life had worn her out. Funny how a little face paint and a few women from her past could whip her back into shape.

"Mama, when you were my age, what did you want?" It was silly to talk to a ghost of the past. It was more foolish to talk to herself and think of her mother at thirty-two and what she'd wanted. The only word Brie could come up with was happiness. Wasn't that what everyone wanted? Life, in its purest form, was simple.

All she needed was a purpose, which usually meant a project, and she had that with The Kessler Resort. But she also needed love and affection, which she was getting from all the people around her, especially Carter. She wanted to feel safe, and thus far, no one had given her a reason to believe they didn't have her best interests at heart. For the first time in as long as she could remember, she felt what she hoped her mama had—happy.

Looking at herself in the mirror, she said, "You're one lucky girl." She changed into the dress and heels and returned to the kitchen.

"Yep, the blue works." Marybeth tucked the green camouflage dress back into her purse. "My job here is done."

Charlotte picked up her makeup. "Mine too." She kissed Brie on the cheek. "You sample all you want and pay no mind to Marybeth. She'll be praying for you, regardless."

Brie laughed. "Good to know."

Both women left, and Brie sat and enjoyed a quiet cup of coffee with Tilly and Em.

"Did someone really win the lotto at the Five and Dime?" Tilly asked.

"Yes, but no one knows who," Em said.

Tilly filled everyone's cups. "If it was me, I'd buy that restaurant in town and name it Edelweiss."

Em looked crestfallen. "You'd leave us?"

Tilly frowned. "I've been here all my life, and I think I'm ready for a new challenge."

Em sat up. "I thought you loved it here."

"I do, but this is yours. It would be nice to have something that's mine one day."

"I understand," Em said, but Brie wasn't sure she did.

Getting away from Willow Bay had been a good thing. It made her appreciate what she was outside of the community, but she also realized how important everyone was to her now that she was back.

Tilly and Em's friendship was also a love relationship. They were like sisters. The longer you stayed with people, the more dependent you became on them. Maybe Carter leaving her had been a good thing. She lived autonomously, made choices and mistakes, and learned from them. If she'd stayed in Willow Bay, all her choices would have been gone. She would have lived up to the expectations of her family. Her dreams would have been set aside to follow the dream of her great grandfather who was dead set on having the best resort in town. Living her dreams was something her aunt had never done, and neither had Tilly. They'd followed another's path. "When was the last time you left Willow Bay?"

"Leave?" Tilly said. "Why would we do that?"

"Because there's more to life than Willow Bay," Brie said.

Em covered Tilly's hand with hers. "No, there isn't." She reached over and grabbed Brie's, too. "Everything I need is right here." She turned to Tilly. "You want an Edelweiss? Let's give you one." They discussed changing the restaurant and eventually settled on theme nights, which would bring Tilly a much-needed challenge. Brie loved the way the two negotiated. That's the way friends and partners should behave. They put their differences on the table and settled them amicably. She hoped she could have that kind of relationship with Carter. They could do anything if they used common sense and compassion.

"Looks like it's time for my hair appointment." She rose from the table and kissed both women on the cheek. "Have fun tonight. What's the town saying about summer?"

"Tomorrow starts one hundred days of stupid," they said together.

CORMAC MCCLINTOCK and Brie crossed paths at Dolly's Doo's; she was going in and he was coming out. "You're looking mighty dapper with your new haircut. Got a date?"

Cormac blushed. "I wish." He was no longer the lanky kid everyone had picked on, but he was still the quiet type who preferred the shadows.

"Surely there's someone you like in town."

He shoved his hands in his pockets. "Sure, but she doesn't know I'm alive."

"Go tell her."

"I have something to do." His expression got all serious. "Do you know if Carter is going to sell the resort?" He shuffled his feet. "I'm asking for a friend."

That was the second time today someone had asked that question. "I don't know. We haven't talked much about it. I can tell him you're interested."

Cormac shook his head. "It's for a friend."

"Right." Cormac had grown up on a nearby ranch, so she wasn't aware of his financial situation, but in her mind, ranchers did decently. "I'll have him call you."

Dolly was waiting for her. "Girl, we don't have all day, and you need a lot of work."

"Don't mess up my makeup."

Dolly led her to the washbowl to shampoo her hair. "I know. Charlotte already called and threatened me to within an inch of my life." She laid Brie back and washed her hair.

"Is Cormac rich?"

Dolly laughed so hard her bosom shook against Brie's side. "That boy doesn't have two nickels to rub together. If he did, he'd be quite the catch. He's sweet and kind and a gentleman. Why? Are you tossing Carter aside already?"

"I was wondering why he asked about Carter selling the property."

"That is odd. I can't imagine a cowboy wanting to lasso rental boats and loungers."

"He said it was for a friend."

"Cormac doesn't have friends." Dolly rinsed Brie's hair and wrapped a towel around it before taking her to her station.

"Why is that?"

"Because nice guys always finish last. Don't you know that?"

She spent the next hour getting her hair cut, curled, and sprayed, but she kept thinking about what Dolly had said. *Nice guys always finish last.* Was that why Carter was still single?

EIGHTEEN

Here made sure everything was ready, from the wine to the music to the flickering battery-operated candles. Real candles would have been sexier, but open flames in an old wooden building weren't wise. He wanted to set Brie's senses on fire, not the boathouse.

The platform he'd built overlooked the bay, giving them a bird's-eye view of the water parade. They'd be able to see everything, tucked into the rafters one story up.

He'd set up what looked like a lover's getaway, filled with luxurious pillows and soft throws. This was his second chance at his first and only love, and he would not blow it.

As the sun set, he checked his phone. This was it. It was redemption time.

STANDING on the porch of her bungalow, he held her favorite flowers. She wasn't a roses kind of girl. She loved yellow daisies mixed with purple irises. He remembered her explaining they were a perfect match because they were across from each other on the color wheel. It made him think about how opposites attract. He'd never considered them opposites, but in hindsight, Brie had always been the light to his darkness.

He knocked and waited. When she opened the door, he nearly fell over. "Wow! You... look... just wow."

She smirked. "Was I less *wow* yesterday?"

Women were tricky, and he didn't want to ruin the date before it started by saying the wrong thing. "You are a ten every day, but today you're a twenty, and it has nothing to do with how you look or what you wear." It was hard to believe this woman could be his by the end of the night, and he wasn't talking about between the sheets. That thought had crossed his mind, but getting into Brie's heart was far more important.

"No?"

"Your beauty comes from who you are as a person. You are kind and caring." And also forgiving because she was here giving him a second chance. "I can't believe we're going on a date."

Her eyes sparkled with delight. "And you remembered my favorite flowers. They're beautiful." She took them inside. "Do you want to come in for a minute?"

He smelled her perfume, and a wave of emotions overwhelmed him, bringing back memories of their past. "If you don't mind, I'd like to start our date. I feel like I've been waiting a lifetime for it."

"I'll just put these in water." When she returned, she glanced at the sweater hanging over a chair. "Will I need it?"

"I'll keep you warm." He brushed his lips across hers. She fell into him and deepened the kiss. Brie tasted like home. Like sunshine and happiness and mimosas on the beach. She was everything he wanted. He hoped he could prove he was everything she needed. Alone they were fine, but together they would be great. He reluctantly pulled away. "Shall we?"

She closed the door behind her. "You lead, and I'll follow."

On the veranda of The Brown Resort were Em, Tilly, Charlotte, and Marybeth, gazing fondly at them like proud parents. It was like prom night all over again. They walked past the crowded beach. He'd set up barriers at the Kessler dock, so people weren't tempted to trespass and do what he was doing—grab a pristine location to view the Parade of Lights.

"Hey," a boy called from the beach. "Why do you get to go inside?"

Carter chuckled. "Because I own it." Then he considered how rude that might have sounded and added, "The boathouse needs repairs before it's ready for the public."

The kid refused to let it go. "Then why does she get to go?"

Carter squeezed Brie's hand. "She's my partner and design consultant."

The kid lowered himself to the sand with a huff and crossed his arms. "Grownups have all the fun."

They went down the dock and into the boathouse. "We're upstairs." He guided her up the steps, where candles flickered and more of her favorite flowers were set in small vases around the room.

"Wow, grownups do have all the fun." She turned in a circle.

He tried to see the space through her eyes—those of a woman who appreciated color and style.

"You did all this for us?"

"No, I did all of this for *you*." Along with the candles, pillows, and throws, he'd tucked fairy lights into the curtains hanging from the rafters. "Is it too much?"

She strolled the perimeter of the landing he'd built, her hand skimming the fabric and making it ripple. "It's perfect." She sank to the floor and lay back on the cushions.

This was everything he could ever want. She was stretched out like she was offering herself to him. "Are you hungry?"

She nodded and smiled. "I am but not for food. Join me?" She patted the space beside her. He was glad they were on the same page.

He settled next to her and pulled her close. "I can't believe we're here and together." He gazed into her eyes and cupped her cheek. "We are together, right?"

"We are here, and we are together," she repeated.

He brushed her cheek with his thumb and thought of all the ways this night could go right or wrong. He didn't want to rush her, but his resolve was weak around Brie. He'd respect her boundaries, of course, but did she want what they'd once had? They'd already wasted a dozen years apart, but his feelings had never changed. Thoughts of her marriage flooded his mind; she also belonged to David.

"Do you miss him?" He put his hands behind his head and leaned back on the pillow.

She immediately tucked herself into his side and laid her head on his chest. "I suppose this is a conversation we need to have."

He dropped his arms and pulled her tightly against him. "It's not. We don't have to discuss it. We talked about it over schnitzel. I was just curious."

She looked up, and all he could see were her eyes, filled with warmth and compassion.

"I don't want to be with you if somewhere deep inside you feel like I'm still with him. He will always live in my heart. He was a good man. Kind. Generous. Loving. But he's gone. My anniversary dinners and endless one-sided conversations were symptoms of my loneliness. It was my way of connecting with the past, but memories can't sustain us. We have to move forward. That's what David would want for me. It's what I want for myself." She kissed his jaw. "You're what I want. I'm not the girl you left years ago, and you're not the man who hurt me. Our experiences make us who we are and who we become. I'm stronger and wiser, and in many ways, happier because of them. I've had two loves in my life, and both caused me terrible pain, but they also gave me great joy. You can't know pure bliss until you've experienced utter devastation."

"I'm so sorry I hurt you."

Her hand settled on his chest and moved in a soft caress. "I've learned to appreciate the force of the universe, and when things aren't right, they don't work."

"Where are we now? Should we start at the beginning?"

"We've already had a beginning and an end." She shifted and moved up to place her lips next to his. "What do you say we start in the middle and write a new story?"

NINETEEN

When Brie's lips touched his, he sighed. When she angled her mouth to deepen the kiss, lava-like heat surged through her. She remembered days filled with friends and nights of stolen kisses in this boathouse. Nothing else mattered but them. Tonight felt the same. Her adult brain required satisfaction for the needs that hadn't been met in years. The teenager inside her, the one who still loved Carter, wanted the time they'd never had. She wanted the passion and playfulness that had been denied.

"Are you sure you want to start in the middle?" he asked. "I've waited a dozen years. I can wait longer."

"Haven't we waited long enough?" She straddled him and looked into his hooded eyes. They weren't the eyes of the Carter of yesteryear, but those of a man who'd experienced a lot of pain in his life. She'd been part of that pain, but it was time to erase it—make fresh memories to override that hurt and finish the love story they'd started.

It took little convincing as he possessively clutched her waist. Even if she tried to get away, his grip was so firm, her efforts would've been futile. Luckily, he locked her in the spot she wanted. He repeatedly stroked her from knees to shoulders with slow and purposeful movements. "You are beautiful. You've always been pretty, but the years have turned you into a true beauty."

She laughed. "Tell that to my beauty consultants who complain incessantly about my skin and my bones."

His hands dropped to her bottom and squeezed. "I like all of you." His hand slipped around to her tummy. "I can think of a lot of ways to fatten you up." He shifted his hips, and she could feel his desire. "But maybe we should start with food."

One moment she was straddling him, and the next, she was on her feet. Disappointment coursed through her, but she had to admit she was hungry. "You're right. Let's eat."

He moved toward the edge of the platform, where he offered her a seat with a million-dollar view. Below, the water lapped at the dock. In the distance, flickering lights hugged the shore and moved closer. "Nothing fancy here, but I got Cricket's fried chicken and stuff." He opened a cooler and arranged their plates.

"You really are trying to fatten me up." This was one of her favorite meals.

"I bought pie, too, in case you needed some sweetening."

She giggled. "I suppose I'm not sweet enough on my own."

He sat across from her. "You're sweet enough for me."

She pointed to the first boat to round the bend. "It's starting." As a kid, she'd never missed the Parade of Lights. The annual event started the hundred days of summer. It was the busiest weekend at the resort, but her parents had always taken time to watch the parade. But she and Carter weren't the only thing that had changed. "Am I imagining things, or have they upped their game?" The first boat to pass was decked out in thousands of lights and a Centennial Celebration banner. At the helm stood the current Miss Lone Star, wearing her crown and a string bikini, her smile as blinding as a searchlight.

"This is next level," he said. "Did you see the work on the American eagle? I wonder how many lights that took?"

"Amazing," was all she could say. He built them a perch that made it seem like the parade was a private viewing. The people on the boats could see them if they looked up but all other viewers seemed to disappear.

"Check out the next one," Carter said enthusiastically. An old sailboat was decked out to resemble a pirate ship.

"Ahoy, mate," the captain said, waving at them. "Can you point me to the treasure?"

Carter pointed at Brie. "This is my treasure; you'll have to find your own."

A string of plastic beads moved through the air and landed on the table. "That's what I have to offer for your beauty," the pirate said.

Brie put the necklace on. "I'll have you know, sir, I can't be bought for baubles."

"She's a sassy one," he said, and the schooner sailed on.

She enjoyed the meal as they watched the parade, but she couldn't help thinking about the past. "You never fell in love again?" she asked, eating Cricket's pie.

He appeared to be startled by the question. "For me, there was only you."

"But you left." This probably wasn't the time to bring it up again, but she wanted to move forward and the not knowing hung in the air like smog. Being young and afraid didn't entirely ring true. The Carter she'd known had always been fearless. He was holding something back.

When she had looked at herself in the mirror earlier, she was all in, so why was she asking questions she knew would put space between them? She had a choice to make—let it go or dig deeper. The former would get her back to the middle, where she knew in her heart they belonged. The latter would rock the boat.

He hung his head. "I will regret that day for the rest of my life."

"I believe you, and I think I owe it to us to let it go. We can't live in the past." She finished her pie and pushed the paper plate aside. She was ready to find out what the middle had in store for her.

The last boat approached, and a gust of wind caught the plate and lifted it into the air. She lunged for it but missed. Carter leaned out to grab it, and his chair toppled. He reached for her but only grasped the beads before plummeting over the edge of the platform.

It happened in slow motion: the fall, the sound of Carter hitting the water, and then the boat's hull. A woman's screaming split the air. Taking the stairs two at a time, she arrived at the dock. The woman's screams didn't stop. That's when she realized it was her.

Several people jumped from the boat into the water. She scoured the surface, looking for him. Swimmers searched the water only to go below and come back empty-handed.

Brie kicked off her shoes and dove in. She was an excellent swimmer. Carter was, too, so the only way he wouldn't come up was if he were unconscious or worse ... dead.

This couldn't be happening. They'd just gotten together. They were supposed to be moving on, but she was here alone. Panic-stricken, she dove again, reaching blindly. She had to find him. She couldn't imagine life without him now that she had him back. Others showed up to shine their lights upon the water. Ten feet down, in the murky depths, she glimpsed shiny gold beads.

She swam deeper, reaching for him. Her lungs were ready to

burst, but if she went up for air, she'd never find him again. She ignored the searing burn in her chest and the lightheadedness. She didn't care. If she couldn't save him, then what was there to live for? She'd lost so much already. Surely the universe wouldn't be so cruel to her twice.

Please help me.

The tips of her fingers came into contact with his body. With a surge of newfound strength, she gripped his shirt and yanked him from the floor of the bay, shooting like a geyser toward the surface.

Once there, she towed him to the shore. "Call 911," she yelled, but her voice was barely there. She felt for his pulse, but it was gone. She shook all over.

On her knees, she administered CPR. People were everywhere, but no one helped her. She sucked in a breath and choked. How was she supposed to breathe for both of them when she couldn't breathe for herself?

The crowd suffocating her divided, and like an angel, Dr. Robinson appeared. She made quick work of doing CPR, and within seconds, Carter was spewing water and choking. Out of nowhere, a blanket was draped over her shoulders, and Aunt Em whispered in her ear, "He'll be okay."

Brie wrenched herself free and threw herself at Carter. "You promised you'd never leave me again."

A weak smile lifted his lips. "I'm going to keep you forever, and one day you'll stand under that willow tree and say 'I do.'"

"Is that a proposal?" She held his hand. "Because if it is, I'll say yes as long as you promise to stay."

He cupped the back of her head and pulled her down for a wet kiss. "Don't tease a man who just faced death, Brie."

She collapsed and laid her head on his chest. "I'm already yours. I always was."

"You can plan the wedding later," Dr. Robinson said. "Right now, you need stitches and x-rays."

Brie bolted upright. She hadn't noticed the gash on Carter's head, but she could see the deep cut and her eyes followed the trail of blood to the sand.

In the distance, the wail of a siren got louder as the ambulance drew closer. "Don't you die on me, Carter Kessler. Our willow tree is waiting."

The paramedics arrived and put Carter on a gurney. Brie followed him to the ambulance. Just before they closed the door, he lifted his head. "Were you serious? Will you marry me?"

"Yes." The doors closed, and Carter was taken away.

An arm went around her shoulders. "Let's get you changed and to the hospital," Em said. "On the way, you can tell me what you want your wedding to look like." She was, among other things, the resort's wedding planner.

Brie's head swam. Could it be true? Was she really marrying Carter? She waited for dread and unease to churn inside her—a warning telling her she was making a mistake—but there wasn't anything. Her soul knew this was right.

TWENTY

"She said yes." Carter looked at the ceiling of the ambulance and smiled. "She said yes, right? I know I hit my head pretty hard—"

"Relax, buddy. I heard it, too. Congrats." The paramedic pressed gauze to Carter's wound. "How long have you known each other?"

Carter smiled. "Forever."

"Feels that way sometimes, right?"

He shook his head and winced at the pain. It used to be that only his heart ached, but tonight he felt like he'd taken a beating, and his heart was the only thing that felt good, and not just regular good but bursting at the seams, overflowing with happiness good. "I've known her since she was born." He closed his eyes and thought back to the day the Browns brought her home. He'd only been two, but he still remembered.

"Open your eyes! You need to stay awake."

Right, he had a head injury. He lifted a hand to touch it, but the medic stopped him. He glanced at the guy's name tag. "How bad is it, Miles?"

"You'll need stitches, and you have a lump the size of Texas, but as long as the inside of your skull looks okay, I think you'll make it." He wrapped gauze around Carter's head and taped it down. "Tell me about your girl."

Carter wanted to laugh but knew it would hurt, so he smiled instead. Calling Brie a girl was funny because she was a grown woman, but seeing as Miles was probably in his fifties, he could see why Miles would call her that. "I almost married her a dozen years ago, but it didn't work out, and we lost touch."

"What brought you back together?"

He knew Miles didn't give a hoot about them; he was doing his job to keep Carter awake and alive until they got to the small medical center at the edge of town. Talking about Brie almost made him forget the pain. "Her Aunt Em's crow's feet."

"Emma Brown? Your fiancée is Emma Brown's niece?"

He nodded, and it felt like a dagger had pierced his brain. "You know her?"

"Emma, yes. Your girl, no. I had a major crush on Em way back, but we weren't meant to be. I'm a McClintock."

He said McClintock like it was a dirty word. "Related to Cormac?"

Miles sat taller. "He's my nephew."

"Does your family still own that ranch outside of town?"

"They do. I left the ranch a long time ago."

Carter sensed there was tension in the McClintock clan, and family drama was something he understood. The twelve-year separation from his father was something he'd always regret. There would be no closure.

"Did you know my father?"

Miles studied him. "Who's he?"

"Cyrus Kessler."

"I knew Cyrus way back when. I heard about you and how you ran, leaving that poor girl under the willow tree. And that's the woman you're marrying now? Boy, you're lucky. If I was her, I'd knock you upside the head." His expression changed. "I don't know what you were thinking."

"I wasn't thinking. If I had been, I'd already be married to Brie and have a few kids by now."

"Well, you can't go back, can you? The past is past, but you can build a new future, which brings me to the next point. I was hoping to meet you. I asked Cormac to set up a meeting."

Carter was having a hard time keeping his eyes open, but he did his best to focus. "You did? Why?"

"I've been saving up and wondered if you might sell the resort."

"It needs a lot of work. It's a money pit, and you'd be married to the job."

"I've always wanted to be married to something. That resort gets me closer to my goal."

"What about what you do now?"

"I'm ready for a divorce. This job is hard on the body and not going in the direction I want to be. I'm looking for the ideal location to plant roots." Miles leaned in and whispered. "I can pay cash."

Carter felt that the resort being on the beach wasn't the location he was talking about. Something told him that crush from long ago had never gone away. "I think Brie and I will keep it, but we haven't talked about it yet." He considered what he said to Miles. The resort was like a lover. It demanded full attention. Did he want that? Would Brie?

The ambulance pulled to a stop, and Miles sat back and waited for his partner to open the door.

"Let's get you inside. I'm sure Dr. Robinson is waiting with her sutures ready." Miles chuckled. "You're the first of no doubt many for the hundred days. I wonder if she'll even numb you before she begins." He laughed. "Just kidding, she probably will."

Miles and his partner wheeled Carter inside. Dr. Robinson leaned over him. "I knew I'd be seeing someone tonight, but I was surprised it was you." He was taken to an exam room and transferred to a bed. Miles went over his vitals and told her about him dozing during the ride. "He's obviously got a hard head."

Fifteen minutes later, Carter was stitched up and getting x-rays. All he could think about was Brie saying yes.

BRIE AND EM were waiting when he got back. Dr. Robinson said he had a concussion but no skull fracture. He'd have to take it easy for a few days, and someone needed to stay with him and watch for slurred words or confusion.

"I'll stay," Brie said. She moved to his side and took his hand. "I'll take care of him."

Em clapped her hands. "Now that's settled, is two weeks from Saturday good for the wedding?" Everyone looked at her. "It's the only free day I've got."

"You two are going through with it this time?" Doc Robinson asked.

He looked into Brie's eyes. Everything she felt was there: worry, hope, love. "It took a hit to the head, but we're finally back where we belong."

"How did you take a header off that deck?" Doc asked.

Carter groaned. "I was chasing a paper plate the wind caught. I didn't want it to land in the water. Bad for the environment."

Doc sighed. "Next time, let it go." She helped him into a sitting position. "You're free to go but take it easy. This could have turned out so much worse." She handed him a prescription. "This is a prophylactic measure and should help with the wound and your lungs. I'd hate to save you from drowning, only to lose you to pneumonia." She helped him to his feet. "I expect an invitation to the wedding."

Miles was filling out paperwork. Carter approached him as they walked out. "Thank you for everything."

"Yes," Brie said. "Thank you."

Carter glanced at Em, who was texting. "Em, do you remember Miles? I think you went to school together."

Her eyes lifted, and she dropped her phone. Miles rushed over to pick it up. "Emmaline," he said in a rich baritone. "It's good to see you again."

She gazed at him in silence, her cheeks turning crimson. "Do I know you?"

Miles chuckled. "You used to, but I've been away for a long time."

"Why don't you join us for supper on Sunday. We dine at The Brown at six." Brie said.

"Oh, heavens, we don't have time to entertain," Em said. "We've got a wedding to plan."

Carter said, "We'll see you at six."

"I'll try to be there."

Em huffed and grunted on the way to the car. "Why did you invite him to dinner?"

Brie opened the door and helped Carter inside before sitting beside him. Em got behind the wheel and turned the key.

"What's wrong with Miles?" Brie asked.

Em growled. "Everything is wrong with that man."

Carter laughed, though it hurt his head. "I thought you didn't know him."

Em sat straighter like she was readying herself for battle. "I know of him."

"Uh-huh," Brie said. "Sounds like there's a story there."

Carter leaned against Brie. "I know there is."

"You two don't get to meddle in my life. There's nothing between Miles and me. He left town a long time ago. I didn't even know he was back."

"Don't talk to me about meddling. You told me you had the Big C."

Em slammed on the brakes and turned around. "It was a little white lie. Can you actually still be mad at me? Look at you two. You're back together and about to get married."

Carter grimaced in pain from the jolt, but he wasn't angry one bit about how things had turned out. He also wasn't the one who'd sold a house, left a job, and buried a lifetime of memories because of a lie. He looked at Brie. "But don't you think it worked out for the best?"

"Getting me here brought me back to you, but how she did it is still awful. Plus, she had no way of knowing how it would turn out." She glared at her aunt. "Not to mention me thinking you had cancer. I was worried sick, so don't talk to me about meddling. There's something between you and Miles, and I aim to figure it out."

Em reached back and patted Brie's knee. "Oh, baby girl. There are some things we choose to remember and some things we have to forget. Sometimes the past is better left in the past." A horn honked. Em rolled down her window and flipped off the driver speeding past. "They need to drink some act right juice." Em faced forward and drove on.

After they pulled into the resort parking lot, Em said, "I'll have Hugh bring your things over to The Kessler tomorrow."

"Thanks," Brie said.

They all climbed out and Em went to her place, and Carter led Brie to his. "He still likes her."

"How do you know?"

"He told me." He cocked his head. "He didn't exactly say it, but he said he had a crush on her when they were young, and it seemed like it never went away." They stood on the porch. It was a beautiful location, but he'd seen what it had done to his parents. All they'd ever done was work and fight, and when Dad wasn't doing that, he was with Brie's mother. "He wants to buy The Kessler."

"He what?" Brie looked at him wide-eyed. "Would you sell it?"

He nodded. "I don't want to be married to the resort. I want to be married to you." He kissed her. "All my life, all I ever wanted was you."

"What would we do?"

He smiled. "Anything we want. Do you have any idea how much this place is worth?" He didn't know how much money Miles had saved, but he had to know that a property like this was worth millions.

Carter opened the door and swept Brie into his arms.

She burst out in laughter. "What are you doing?"

He kissed her again. A deep, slow kiss that silenced her. "I'm carrying my fiancée to bed."

"You're going to hurt yourself, or worse, kill yourself."

He carried her inside and closed the door. "Maybe, but I'll die a happy man."

TWENTY-ONE

"Put me down before you injure yourself." He carried her through the living room to his bedroom. She hadn't been there in over a decade, but it hadn't changed one bit. The living room still had that Hawaiian island feel, and when they entered his bedroom, she was transported back in time. "It's like a shrine." He set her gently on the full-sized bed.

"My parents didn't touch a thing after I left. They cleaned around it."

Bookshelves held his trophies, with pictures of them together interspersed. She rose and picked up their engagement photo, taken under the willow tree. "We were so young then."

Carter sat on the edge of the bed and tugged her back until she was sitting beside him, photo in hand. "But we knew we belonged together."

She'd never forget her time with David. She'd loved him with all the heart she had left, and he loved her, too, but their love differed from what she had with Carter. A piece of her could never belong to anyone but him because their love was celestial, the kind that was written in the stars long before they were born. Her love for David had been one of need.

She set the photo to the side. "How are you feeling?"

"Better than I have in a dozen years." He lay back, taking her with him.

"No, I mean your head."

He moved up until his head was on a pillow and summoned her with a curl of his finger. She followed until they were side by side, with her head on his chest. His clothes were still damp but felt good against her cheek.

"It's just a bump." He kissed the top of her head. "I'll live."

"It's ten stitches, and you better live because I'm not burying another husband."

"We're not married yet."

Brie rubbed his chest. "We are in my heart."

"I'm sorry I ruined our night."

She sat up. "You didn't. I've always loved you, but I had no idea how strong my feelings were until you went over the edge, and I couldn't find you."

His eyes grew wide. "You found me?"

"I thought you knew. I ran down the stairs, and when you didn't surface, I dove in."

"You saved my life in more than one way tonight, Brie. I've been drowning for years, and only you could rescue me." He shivered.

"Let's get these damp clothes off." She pulled on the hem of his shirt until she met resistance. Stalling, she took a minute to appreciate his body. The line of hair leading from his sculpted abs to the waistband of his pants and lower underscored that he wasn't the boy she'd made love to. This was a man whose hard work had honed his body to perfection. His broad chest used to be bare, but now had a smattering of dark hair.

"Are you done ogling?" He removed his shirt and tossed it.

"Nope, I think I'll drool over you a while longer." She skimmed his chest with her fingertips. That light touch sent a tingle up her arm and down her spine. It had been over five years since she'd made love. Five years since a man had touched her. Since she'd felt much of anything. "Pants next." She unbuttoned and unzipped and yanked at the waist until they were down below his narrow hips. "You look better than ever."

He kicked off his shoes and shimmied out of his pants. This was her future husband, and it almost felt like déjà vu. But this time they were older and wiser and ready for love.

Carter always looked like he lived at the beach, with his bronze skin and sun-bleached hair.

When she stroked his arm, tiny bumps rose on his skin. "Are you cold?"

"No, baby, I'm burning up."

Her hand went straight to his forehead. "Fever?"

"Nope. Passion."

The desire between them was undeniable. She knew where this was going. "Do you think this is wise?"

"I don't want to think. All I want to do is feel." He took off her shirt. "I had a plan." Her jeans came off next. She'd been in such a hurry to change and get to the hospital, she hadn't put on undergarments. The cool air was a welcome relief to the fire inside her.

"You had a plan?" she whispered.

"I did, but it looked nothing like this." He couldn't take his eyes off her. "I'd fall off a building every day if it ended like this." He pulled her close, and the hairs on his chest tickled her sensitive skin.

"Tell me about it." She fell to her side, taking him with her. Their legs intertwined, and they explored all the places they'd been denied with hands and lips.

He nipped at her mouth and then followed the gentle bite with a kiss. "Dinner." He nibbled again, drawing her bottom lip between his and sucking it for several seconds before letting it pop free. "The parade." He reached behind her and flattened his hand against her back. "I brought all those cushions and pillows."

"I noticed. It's a shame we didn't get to enjoy them longer."

"I hoped to woo you."

"You were going to woo me?" She quivered in his embrace, thinking about all the possibilities. "What would that have looked like?"

"Long, slow kisses and soft, tender caresses."

"That's a good start." She inched her finger into the band of his boxers. "Were there plans to get naked?"

"No, but I was open to suggestions." He assisted in the removal of his boxers, and they touched what they could reach but didn't take it further.

"Tell me how you planned to kiss me." His mouth came to hers, but he didn't kiss her.

"My lips on yours, soft at first, and then deeper until you make those noises I used to love."

She worked one leg between his thighs. "What noises were those?"

"Let me show you." His hand went to her head, holding her in place while he made love to her mouth. And she made noises—soft whimpering sounds that revealed her need.

"Yep, those are the ones, but my favorite is the sound you make when we become one. It's like you've been waiting for me forever." He shifted until she was above him "Are you ready for forever, Brie? I know we've done this before, but this is different. This is our chance to take everything we've learned and put it to work making a lifetime of happiness."

She moved above him. "Shut up and make love to me." The

words were more begging than demanding. "Aren't you tired of waiting?"

He aligned his hips with hers. "The wait was torture, but the reward was so sweet." He slid into her body, and she sighed like he was all she needed for the rest of her life.

TWENTY-TWO

A splitting headache woke him. At first, Carter wanted to die because he was halfway there already. But he was getting married in two weeks, and that healed every ache he'd ever experienced.

He reached for Brie, but the bed beside him was empty. Had he dreamed last night? Dr. Robinson said he had a concussion, but surely, he wasn't in bad enough shape to imagine the best night of his life. It was like the wedding night he'd wished for all those years ago, only better.

"Brie?" He rolled to a sitting position, but the throbbing in his temple insisted he lay back down. "Are you here?" He stared at the ceiling as the scent of her perfume rose from the pillowcase.

"Be right there," she called from the kitchen. The soft tap of her feet on the wooden floors brought him comfort. When she came in wearing his T-shirt and boxers, all the pain disappeared, and he was ready for more. "I had a tough time figuring out the coffeepot, but I think I got it." She held two cups in her hand. "All you have is cereal, so I asked Tilly to make us breakfast. She'll send Hugh over with a tray soon."

He patted the space beside him. "Come back to bed."

She laughed. "If I climb into that bed, we may never leave it." She sat on the edge beside him and placed his coffee on the nightstand, then checked his forehead for fever.

"I'm fine. I'm better than fine. I feel..." There weren't adequate words to describe this emotion. He was happy, but it was in a way he'd never been before. Even when they were kids, he'd never experienced this. Maybe it was because he had perspective. It was easier to feel joy when he knew what emotional annihilation was. "I feel whole."

"I do too." She sipped her coffee. "But how's the head?"

He reached for her coffee and set it next to his before pulling her to him. "Do I look like a man who's hurting?"

"I know you're hurting. I also know you're stubborn and will ignore it if you think there's a chance of us making love again." She gave him a pointed look.

"Is there a chance?"

They lay side by side, facing each other. "You're insatiable."

He nibbled at her lip. "I'm making up for lost time."

"If that's the case, we won't leave this room for a long while."

"And what's wrong with that?"

She moved closer. "Nothing at all."

THEY EMERGED THIRTY MINUTES LATER, not because they wanted to, but because Hugh wouldn't stop knocking.

"Can I kill him?" he asked.

"That man's a national treasure." She jumped out of bed and

put his boxers and T-shirt back on before rushing to answer the door.

Carter moved slower than Brie, but he pulled on a pair of sweatpants and a T-shirt before going to the dining room, where Hugh was setting up their breakfast. He'd come equipped with everything, from silverware to cloth napkins and those fancy crystal salt and pepper shakers. After he finished, Hugh stood and waited. Carter couldn't figure out what he was waiting for, but when Brie grabbed her purse, the light dawned. She handed him a tip.

"Have a nice day," Hugh said and left.

"I can't believe he expected you to tip him." He pulled out a chair at the table for his fiancée. There was only one word that was better than that—wife.

"He's doing his job and expects to get paid."

He sat next to her. "If he gets ten dollars for every delivery, he's making bank, and I'm in the wrong line of work."

Brie lifted both cloches to reveal eggs, bacon, and fried potatoes. Toast and biscuits, butter, and jam were in a basket.

"Speaking of work, we have decisions to make. Do you really want to sell the resort?"

He buttered a biscuit and dipped it into the yolk of one egg. "As my partner, we should decide together."

She chewed a piece of bacon, thinking. "It's been in your family for generations. Can you let go of it so easily?"

"It would be difficult, but I don't want to see what happened to our parents happen to us. I don't want the resort to be the focus of our life."

She nodded. "What about our children? "

He hadn't thought about that. "You want children?"

She paled. "Maybe we should have talked about that before we had unprotected sex last night."

"It was unprotected?"

"I haven't been with anyone for years. There was no need. Please don't tell me you're dead set against kids."

He took her hand. "When I touched your stomach and told you there were other ways of fattening you up, I wasn't talking about donuts. "

She smiled. "You want more than one?"

He wanted at least two, but he'd take as many as they could make together. "Being an only child wasn't so fun. I want our children to have accomplices when they get into mischief and friends when no one else can come out and play."

She squeezed his hand. "I agree. We had each other, but not everyone gets to live next door to their soul mate."

"True. Now, back to the resort. What are you thinking?"

She poured them each a cup of coffee. "I'm on the fence, which means I'm not ready to let this go. While I agree that I don't want to be attached at the hip to the resort, I also don't want to be hasty and sell it." She looked around the room. "Your family is in the woodwork here. While you have every right to move on, make sure you're selling it for the right reasons."

"There are a lot of good and bad memories here."

"Tell you what. We both know the resort could be profitable if it were running at full capacity. We also know that we don't want to sign on for a lifetime of servitude to the business if our hearts aren't in it."

"What are you suggesting?"

"You have an interested party, but it's someone who's never run a resort. Do you suspect Miles' motivation is more about getting near Aunt Em?"

He shrugged. "We had a minute-long conversation. Although it was short, and I had a head injury, I got the distinct impression he was interested in being near Em." He wondered if he should ask the question on the tip of his tongue and then couldn't help himself. "Do you think your grandparents had something to do with what happened between them?"

"Why would they have anything to do with them?"

He took a deep breath. Everything he knew would eventually come out, so it was better to plant the seed now. "Supposedly our parents dated at one time."

Brie choked on a mouthful of food and hastily swallowed. "Which parents?"

He watched her closely. "My dad and your mom."

She laughed. "I've never heard anything so ridiculous. Could you imagine them together?"

"It's not so crazy. Like you and me, they grew up next door to each other."

"You can't believe everything you hear."

"You can't discount it either."

Still quietly chuckling, she said, "Imagining them together is impossible."

"Maybe for you but just open your mind to the possibility. What if they were in love and couldn't be together? It's not an idea that doesn't have merit."

"It's a ridiculous notion. I don't want to imagine it."

He let it go. "Okay, let's get back to the resort. What are you suggesting?"

"Maybe Miles would be interested in managing the property for a time until we decide what to do with it."

"I can't afford to hire a manager." He was on a shoestring budget as it was. "Dad left nothing when he passed."

"I can afford it."

"I can't let you do that."

She frowned. "But you just said we were partners."

"We are, but that's your money from the sale of your house, and it's your nest egg."

"Does that mean if you sold the resort, it would be *your* nest egg?"

"No, what's mine is yours."

"And what's mine is yours. I'll cover Miles's salary until we decide."

This was a fight he wouldn't win. "Deal. Shall I call him?"

TWENTY-THREE

B rie sat at a folding table near the end of the dock, waiting for the next boat to arrive and take a card from her deck. The Harbor Hop was a game of poker, and the boats stopped at several locations to pick up a card for their hand. The rules were simple: the best hand of five cards won. The prize was a portion of the pot of money collected to enter. The biggest prize was never the money. It was bragging rights.

"I could have done this," Aunt Em said as she appeared with two glasses of sweet tea.

"You hate this. Besides, it makes me feel useful since you basically fired me from The Kessler."

"I didn't fire you. I was giving you what you wanted."

"Since when did what I want factor into anything?"

Em sat in the chair beside her. "Did you or did you not get what you wanted? You and Carter are back together. I didn't have to force you together. You figured it out on your own. That's a good thing, right?"

"It's good." Her cheeks heated, and she hoped her already sun-

146

kissed face hid the secret she was keeping. Any talk of Carter sent her straight to the night before, where he'd made love to her repeatedly.

"You're happy then?"

Brie sighed. "I am, but I feel guilty." A boat pulled up to the dock and swiped a card before taking off.

"What have you got to feel guilty about?" Aunt Em moved the cards around so there wasn't an empty space. That seemed to be Aunt Em's superpower—filling voids. It was what she'd done for Brie by bringing her back to Willow Bay. "You're not having second thoughts, are you?"

"Heavens no. I still have many unanswered questions, but I can't focus on the past when I finally have a future. How many people are lucky enough to get a do-over?"

"The past is where it belongs. This isn't a repeat, but a fresh start. Bury your doubts and move on."

"The guilt comes from having two loves in my life and looking at others who have never experienced one. Like you. Have you never been in love?"

Em stiffened. "It's not that I've never been in love. It's that love isn't something that suits me."

"All that means is you haven't found the right person."

"Oh, I found him all right," Em murmured.

"What?" Brie asked, hoping she'd explain.

"I said I found him, but Brad Pitt was already married. Then there was Sting." She rolled her eyes. "I threw my best bra at him at a concert, but it didn't work out between us. Let's forget about me and focus on you. Tilly is making your cake, but she wants to know how many tiers and what filling. Since this is like a shotgun wedding, I have no time to print formal invitations, so I thought we could invite the town via a post in the paper. It's not fancy, but it's inclusive."

"That will work, or we can have a small intimate affair which isn't inclusive because the wedding isn't for anyone but Carter and me."

Em pulled a notepad from her pocket and wrote *intimate affair*. "I like that, and you're right, this is about you and Carter, but I'd be lying if I didn't say it gives the resort a chance to shine."

It was like the resort was a living, breathing being.

"Do you ever regret taking this place on after my parents died?" When Brie's grandparents passed, the resort was handed down to Em and Brie's mother. While her father was an integral part of its success, he had no claim to ownership. When her mother died, her share of the resort was given to Brie, but she left it to her aunt to run because she was out of state. In Brie's mind, she didn't have a claim on any of it.

"The resort is part of who I am. I've never known anything else. Your ancestors sank everything into this property."

"I used to think Carter and I would grow up and run The Kessler, and my family would run The Brown, but being away from it taught me there's more than this."

"It's good you got that time away because the resort is like a jealous lover and will require much attention."

Brie considered Carter's proposal to sell and her counter to keep the resort and hire a manager. "I don't want that for me, so I think we will hire help."

She didn't dare mention Miles's name. It had touched a nerve at the hospital, and Brie wasn't willing to push it again.

"No one will ever do the job you would unless they have skin in the game."

"Then I suppose we'll have to find a person who needs The Kessler as much as we need him or her."

"Good luck with that." Em glanced at her notebook. "Irises and yellow daisies for the wedding flowers?"

Brie nodded. "We can do irises and yellow roses." Her aunt thought daisies were cheap flowers, and she wouldn't want any onlookers to think The Brown Resort had skimped on the bride.

Em smiled. "I love a good compromise."

"Isn't that what life is all about?"

"Not according to your grandparents. They were rigid in their beliefs and goals."

"I know. He who dies with the most wins."

"Can't say I can argue since we own Willow Bay's biggest chunk of land. We didn't get that because Horace Brown was good at sharing." She looked out at the bay and the line of boats on their way to the dock. "You're about to get busy. Don't forget to hand out the brochures. There's no point in doing this if it doesn't bring in business."

"Life isn't all about profits."

Em smiled. "Mine is." She rose and took a few steps. "What about that cake?"

"Two-tier, white with lemon filling." It was what they'd decided on back then, and she was certain Carter didn't care. This time around, she didn't either. All she wanted was to stand in front of the man she'd loved all her life and say "I do."

"And the rings?"

She'd never thought about rings. "Oh my god, I knew we'd forget something."

TWENTY-FOUR

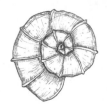

"I don't have a ring," Carter told his mother.

"Sure, you do. Have you gone into the safe?"

"There's a safe?"

"It's hidden under the carpet in the closet. My ring would be there unless your father sold it."

Carter went to his parents' bedroom and opened the safe with the combination she'd given him. He pulled out what looked like ledgers, set them on the nearby table, and then went back inside to find a small jewelry box. He opened it to reveal a single solitaire and a plain gold band. It wasn't ornate, but it was classic and beautiful. "Do you think it's bad luck to give Brie a ring from a failed marriage?"

His mother laughed. "It's not the ring's fault."

"You know what I mean. I don't want to start the second time around with bad juju."

"I'd say you got all that stuff over with on the first round. What's there to stand in your way now?"

"I don't want to ask that question. No good ever came from

borrowing trouble." He pocketed the ring and closed the safe. "You're coming, right? I can get a room ready for you."

"I'll be there. No way am I missing my only child's wedding. And thanks for the offer, but I'm staying at The Brown. Em was nice enough to give us bungalow three since it recently vacated."

He understood why his mother wouldn't want to stay at The Kessler. There were too many memories here. "I get it. Is Frank coming?"

"He wouldn't miss it for the world either. How's the head?"

"Reeling, everything is happening so fast, but it's long overdue."

"I meant the injury."

He'd filled his mother in on the fall and the concussion. "If I didn't have a lump the size of an egg or stitches, I wouldn't even know I'd hurt myself. There are too many things to think about and feel that are good. I'm not focusing on the negative."

"That's great. What's on the agenda for today?"

He tapped his pocket and felt the ring. "I'm going to propose once more. Only I'll do it right this time, down on one knee and ring in my hand."

"If she's the Brie I remember, she won't care about the ring. All she'll care about is—"

"I know. She'll just want me to show up."

"That wasn't what I was going to say. All she cares about is you."

He left the room. "She doesn't seem to be hung up on the past, so I don't know why I am."

"Because it's like a noose, choking you to death. The past is tied to our immaturity and mistakes. It has nothing to do with the future."

"It does if you don't learn from it."

"Are you going to show up?"

He chuckled. "Mom, I'll beat her there, and I won't leave until she arrives, and we're officially married."

"That's the spirit."

He said goodbye and trotted down to The Brown Resort dock, where Brie was giving away the last card from her deck. When she saw him, her smile broadened, and her eyes lit up like the lights he'd hung from the rafters.

"Good afternoon, handsome." She rose. "Did you call Miles?"

He nodded and gestured her back to her chair. "I spoke with him before my mother, and he's interested."

"Awesome! We can hammer out the details tomorrow after brunch."

"He isn't coming. He doesn't want to upset Emmaline." He said Em's name exactly the way Miles had, with a breath and a sigh. Miles had it bad for Em. The Brown women were like a drug that was hard to get out of your system.

"That's too bad. I was hoping to give Aunt Em a little taste of her own medicine."

"I outlined the basics for Miles, and he thought it was a brilliant idea. He also likes that he can try it before he buys it. I thought a good trial would be while we were on our honeymoon. I'll iron out the details next week."

"We get a honeymoon?"

"My mom and Frank are gifting us a trip."

She bounced in her chair. "There are so many things to plan, and a honeymoon wasn't even on my radar."

He dropped to one knee in front of her. "I bet a ring wasn't either."

A woman sitting on the edge of the dock gasped, then punched the man sitting beside her in the arm. "Turn around, Hank. That's how it's done. You don't pop open a beer can and say, 'Let's get hitched.'"

Hank made a face and shrugged. "You said yes anyway."

She shouldered him. "That's because I didn't have other plans that weekend."

Hank glanced at us. "We had a friend marry us in the back-yard twenty years ago, and all it cost was a case of beer. We didn't need fancy, we needed each other."

Hiding a smile, Carter turned away from the couple. "Brie Watkins, this is my second chance to get it right." He pulled the ring out. "I have loved you all my life. I think I fell in love with you the day your mom brought you home. You were all pink and wrinkly, but I thought you were beautiful." He opened the box to show her the rings. "These were my mother's, and she wanted you to have them. She said not to hold the history against the jewelry."

Brie reached out to touch the rings, but Carter pulled them back. "Not yet. There's something I need to ask."

"I already said yes."

"I know, but I was injured and didn't get the full experience."

She giggled. "You realize this will be the third time you've proposed to me?"

"They say third time's a charm." He held her hand. "Brie Watkins, will you marry me and become my wife? Will you grow old with me and share my life?" He placed the solitaire on the tip of her finger and waited.

"I've said yes to you every time you've asked. With you, I don't understand no."

Hank laughed. "Wait until you've been married a while, and no will be your first response to everything."

"Hank, you're ruining a beautiful moment."

Carter smiled, "Brie, I love you, and I always will."

"I love you, too, and yes, I'll marry you." She pushed her finger forward until the ring was in place, and then they kissed to seal the deal. When she pulled back, she looked at the ring on her finger, and he wondered if she was thinking about the one he'd put there before. The yellow diamond surrounded by amethysts hadn't been traditional, yet somehow Brie had convinced the jeweler to take it back because weeks after he left, a credit showed up on his card from the store.

"We can get you something different. I'm happy to do that if you want the yellow diamond and amethysts."

She shook her head. "I'm not that girl anymore."

He pressed his lips to hers. "No, you're wiser, prettier, and you're mine." He rose to his feet. "Are you done here?"

"I am. What did you have in mind?"

He gave her a look he hoped told her precisely what he had in mind. "The loft awaits."

"Promise not to fall over the edge?"

They made use of the cushions and pillows and an hour later, they walked hand in hand to their new home.

Margot exited the lobby. "Oh, Carter." She ran over. "Are you okay?"

"Couldn't be better. We're getting married." He held up Brie's hand to show Margot the ring.

"Wow. How did that happen?"

Brie smiled. "The usual way. He asked, and I said yes."

"Some girls have all the luck," Margot said.

Brie reached out and hugged Margot. "Your prince will come."

Margot laughed. "I hope he drives a white SUV and loves kids."

"It's possible," Carter said. "My grandpa always told me, 'Never kick a cow turd on a hot day.'"

Margot stared at him like he'd lost his wits. "What's that supposed to mean?"

"It means timing is everything." He looked down at his fiancée. "Ready to go home, love?"

TWENTY-FIVE

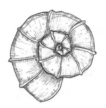

B rie couldn't believe how fast time had flown. Preparation for the wedding kept her busy, and when she wasn't talking about flowers, her dress, or the menu, she was making love to Carter.

"Mom and Frank landed and will be here in about an hour." Carter had been cleaning out the master bedroom so they could move into it on their wedding night. His full-size bed was fine, but this was their home for now, and it was time to make it feel like it.

Brie liked the distraction because her wedding was two days away. Carter would be there this time, but the old fear still reared its ugly head.

"Will she be okay in bungalow three?" Brie asked from the doorway. Carter had banned her from the room, and she didn't dare step inside. He was up to something, and she had a sneaky suspicion it was another lovers' retreat. He'd taken the loft in the boathouse apart because he worried others would find it and take advantage of the space.

"She's excited to be there. She always admired your mother's style."

Brie snorted. "Your mother hated my mother. They were cordial because they were neighbors."

"My mother was jealous," Carter said.

"Of what?"

"Lots of things, I'm sure." He handed her a stack of leather-bound books. "I think these are the ledgers for the business. Can you put them somewhere else, so they don't get lost?"

"There was nothing to be jealous of." She took the books. "If anything, my mother should have been the jealous one."

"Oh, I'm sure it went both ways. You always want what you don't have." He kissed her quickly. "I have errands to run. Do you want to come with me or stay here?"

She was exhausted from the whirlwind of activities the last few days. "I think I'll stay and maybe take a nap."

He kissed her again. "Don't forget we're having dinner at Cricket's with Mom, Frank, and Em at six. I'll be back to pick you up."

"I'll be ready." She set the ledgers on the dresser in his room, then kicked off her shoes and climbed under the blanket. She lay on her side facing the nightstand and saw the journals her aunt had given her. Curious, she picked up one, rolled on her back, and opened it to see what was inside. A tri-folded piece of paper fell to her chest. Closing the book and putting it aside, she picked the paper up. It was old and looked like it had been read a thousand times, judging by the wrinkles and worn edges. The inscription on the front read *To my love.*

Could this be a love letter from her father to her mother? Her parents had never been physically demonstrative, but they'd loved each other. No one stayed married that long without a special bond.

Olivia, My Love,

You are the first thought I have in the morning and the last at night. Our love is complicated, but it's the purest thing I've ever known.

You were born for me, and I for you. The universe got it wrong but somehow made it right. What we have isn't perfect, but it's forever because my heart only beats for you. I feel you close to me even though you're far away. I love you. That will always be true.

Every moment you're not by my side or in my arms is torture.

I always miss you. I always love you.

Yours Forever,

There was no name. Brie read the letter over again. Theirs was a passion so great that any time apart was torture. She wanted that with Carter. The words seemed to be speaking to her directly. *The universe got it wrong but somehow made it right.* Wasn't that what happened to them? They'd screwed it up the first time, but now they got a second chance.

What we have isn't perfect, but it's forever because my heart only beats for you. Even when Carter left her that day on the beach, she knew it wasn't because of another woman. The Kesslers and Browns were loyal, and she couldn't imagine any of them being unfaithful. She folded it and tucked it in her back pocket so she could share it with Carter later.

As she dozed, she pictured her mother reading the letter and how good it must have felt to know she'd married her soul mate.

SHE JOLTED awake at five-thirty and bolted from bed. She hadn't seen Carter's mom in years and didn't want to show up late. She touched up her makeup, brushed her teeth, and wrestled her hair into submission. She considered changing into a dress, but they were going to Cricket's, not the fancy steakhouse on the edge of town, so jeans were appropriate.

Besides, Claudia knew her and wouldn't expect a fuss. Her mom, on the other hand, would. She heard her whispering in her ear, "Get gussied up." She compromised and changed her shirt and shoes. The baby blue lacy number brought out the blue in her eyes, and the wedge sandals dressed up her jeans. She'd just finished spritzing on perfume when Carter appeared.

"You ready?" he asked. "Mom is meeting us there."

"Give me a second. You can't rush perfection." She took a last glance in the mirror and declared herself presentable.

Carter came up behind her and wrapped his arms around her. "You were born perfect for me."

That reminded her of the letter in her pocket. "I found a letter from my father to my mother."

He nuzzled her neck. "That sounds interesting." He kissed her collarbone, then ran his tongue from the hollow there to her earlobe.

"Carter Kessler, you're going to make us late."

"If it were anyone other than my mother, I'd tell them to wait, but she's about to burst a seam, she's so excited to see you." He nuzzled her neck. "Maybe we can be a little late."

She moved away. "I will not get in trouble for keeping your mother waiting."

Em was waiting at his truck. "I thought I'd have to come get you." She grinned at Brie. "You have that just look about you."

"Just what?" Brie climbed into the cab while her aunt sat behind her, in the extended back.

"I'm not going into details. That would require Marybeth to pray for my soul."

"If I have a 'just look' about me, it's because I *just* woke up."

"Is that why your neck is all red?"

Carter chuckled.

Brie pulled down the sun visor. "If you gave me a hickey, you're in trouble." She flipped the mirror to make sure he hadn't left a mark. "You're lucky."

He reached for her hand. "If I had, I'd have been marking you as mine."

Aunt Em laughed. "You sound like a dog. You could have peed on her leg and called it a day."

"You missed your calling. You should have been a comedian," Brie said to Aunt Em.

"Funny doesn't pay the bills."

"Maybe if you took your act on the road," Brie retorted.

"Child, you are talking out your hind end. I have responsibilities that keep me right where I am."

"Are those responsibilities what made you break up with Miles?" Brie asked.

The cab was silent until Em cleared her throat. "If you keep bringing him up, you and I will have a come-to-Jesus meeting."

"Perfect," Brie said. "I'll invite Marybeth, and she can make the introductions." In the visor mirror, she saw her aunt raise her hand, but Carter parked at the perfect time, and Brie hopped out of the cab before being dealt a swift backhand to the head. "I'm starving. Let's go."

She joined Carter on the sidewalk, where he said, "You're playing with fire."

She gave him a quick kiss. "We both are. Did you make a deal with you know who?"

"It's all set."

"I wish I could be here to see it all go down."

"We have other plans. Hawaii calls," Carter said.

"Hawaii?" Em asked as she joined them.

"We figured Maui would be a great place to honeymoon," Brie

said.

Em smiled. "Hawaii sounds perfect."

The minute they stepped inside; a squeal of delight came from the big round booth in the corner.

"Brie Brown, you haven't changed one bit!" Claudia, Carter's mom, rushed forward and hugged her like she hadn't seen her in a lifetime. It did seem about that long.

"It's Watkins, Mom."

Claudia waved dismissively. "It hardly matters since she'll be a Kessler in two days."

A tall man standing next to her offered Brie his hand. "I'm Frank Ricci. It's a pleasure to meet the woman who stole my son's heart."

Brie's heart lurched. Carter had lost his father, but Frank filled the role nicely. Maybe the estrangement hadn't been so difficult for Carter because he'd had a surrogate when the relationship with his real father collapsed. She still didn't know why that happened, but they had a lifetime ahead of them to talk about it.

"He stole mine, too."

Claudia greeted Em and then they all took their seats in the booth.

Cricket arrived with her red high-tops and a grin. "Well, I'll be. I never thought I'd see this day. I'm happier than a woodpecker in a lumberyard. You two getting back together is a miracle." Cricket took their drink order and left.

"They say true love always wins." Claudia leaned on Frank's arm and smiled. Brie thought about love and remembered the letter in her pocket.

"Speaking of love..." She pulled the paper out. "I found this in my mother's things, and since my parents couldn't be with us tonight, I thought I'd bring them here in spirit. It's a love letter. Do you mind if I read it?"

TWENTY-SIX

"I'm all ears. I might even learn something," Carter said.

Em stared at the paper in Brie's hand. "Your father didn't have a romantic bone in his body. His idea of romance was lighting a candle after he passed gas."

Brie giggled. "He definitely did that, but the proof is right here." She read the letter aloud. "Aren't his words sweet?" She turned to Carter. "You were born for me, and I for you. Don't you think that's romantic?"

His mother had gone white, and Carter suddenly knew who the writer of the letter was.

"What do you think, Mrs. Ricci?"

"Call me Claudia, sweetheart. I think the words are heartfelt and true."

Brie looked at her Aunt Em as if asking the same, but she had the expression of a woman who'd eaten a bad meal. "What do you think?"

Em swallowed hard. "I think it's time to order."

Brie looked confused. The letter hadn't had the impact she

expected. She folded it and put it back in her pocket, and everyone relaxed.

"It's a nice letter," Carter whispered. "And yes, I was born for you. It was my job to forge a path for us. I failed once, but I will not fail again."

Cricket arrived with their drinks. "I'm shorthanded tonight, so you'll all be having the special."

"What is it tonight?" Claudia asked.

Cricket shrugged. "I'm not sure, but you're going to love it. If you don't, you don't have to pay. But here's some advice: Tell me you love it, so I won't have to show you the underside of my shoe." She left.

"What does that mean?" Frank asked.

Brie laughed. "She's got a lovely picture drawn on the sole of her shoe for difficult customers." Brie tapped her middle finger on the table until everyone knew what she meant.

"Genius," Em said. "I wonder how many times she's had to use that." Em touched her chin. "I need to get some Sharpies for the front desk."

"How is The Brown running these days?" Claudia gave Brie and Em a sympathetic look. "I'm sorry for your loss."

Em said, "Thank you, but you know as well as I do, I was born to run the resort. We were raised on sweet tea and ledgers. I knew how to make a bed you could bounce a quarter off of before I was potty trained."

"The Kesslers and the Browns were something."

"Certifiable," Em said with a hint of pride.

A few minutes later, Cricket showed up with fried chicken and biscuits. "Eat up and get out. I have a wedding to go to in two days. I need my beauty sleep."

"Don't you work tomorrow?"

Cricket slapped him with her order pad. "I do, but I'm splitting my extra sleep over two days. Since Tilly is cooking for the whole town, I'm closing up shop. It will be the first time I've done that in twenty years."

"What happened then?" Frank asked.

"I got a wild hair up my keister to ride on the back of a Harley. Some cutie came in, and, well..." She winked. "I got a ride, and so did he."

Everyone's mouth dropped open. Claudia must have decided it was time to change the subject. "Did you find the perfect dress, Brie?"

She silently handed the question to Carter, who said, "We didn't want anything formal and fussy. I haven't seen her dress, but I hope it matches the linen pants and shirt I got."

Em raised a hand. "I'm in charge of coordinating, and I can assure you that what you bought works because I sent you the links. As for Brie, she'll look like a goddess in white."

As they ate, the conversation shifted from the wedding to the town, and Em caught everyone up on who was who and what was what. When Cricket flicked the lights off and on, they knew it was time to leave.

Carter tried to pay the bill, but Frank said it was his job to pick up the rehearsal dinner, and since they weren't having a rehearsal, he'd pay for the meal. Carter was happy if this was a preview of how things would play out. Everyone seemed to enjoy themselves. Even the one awkward moment didn't seem so uncomfortable.

They got in their vehicles, only this time Em rode with Carter's mom and Frank, leaving Brie and him alone in the truck.

"Claudia seems happy," she said as they drove home.

"She is. Frank is a good man and gives her what my father couldn't."

"And what's that?"

He didn't know what to say. Telling her the truth would have been like shaking a hornet's nest. He settled on what he hoped was so obscure she wouldn't question it. "All of himself."

After they got home, they made sure his mother and Frank were settled before going to their place. How weird was it for his mother to be back and staying at The Brown? *Probably a lot less weird than staying with Brie and him.*

They watched television for an hour before he faded. "Do you mind if I go to bed? I'm exhausted. I have to be up early to see Dr. Robinson. She's taking out my stitches so I can look sexy on our wedding day."

"You look sexy now." She went to the bedroom with him. "Do you mind if I stay up for a while? Em gave me my mother's gardening and recipe books, and since she's not here, I thought I'd read through them to feel closer to her." She picked up the journals.

"Enjoy." He kissed her deeply. "I love you, Brie." He pulled back from the kiss, lost his balance, and knocked over the ledgers Brie had placed on his dresser.

He started to pick them up, but Brie yelled, "Wait." She reached for a smaller leather-bound book. "This is the same one my mother has."

As Carter took in the journals, fear raced up his spine. "Brie, give me the book." He reached for it, but she stepped back.

"Why?"

Logic told him if her mother and his father had the same journal, it couldn't be good. He noticed the intertwined hearts on the cover and knew he was right. "Just give it to me."

"Why are you acting so strangely?"

"I'm not. Those are my father's things, and I haven't seen them yet. I'd like to spend some time with them on my own before sharing them with you."

She lowered the book, but she didn't offer it to him. "But you share everything. Why not this?"

He pressed his lips so tightly together he couldn't feel them after a few seconds. "Because if I'm right, what's inside will ruin everything we've created."

"What are you talking about?"

"I don't know for sure, but are you willing to risk what we have to find out?"

"I've hidden nothing from you. I refuse to start our marriage with secrets."

"Baby, they aren't our secrets."

"What are you saying?"

He'd been holding on to this secret forever, and she was right. They couldn't start their marriage on a shaky foundation. He blurted, "That letter you read wasn't from your father to your mother. It was from my father to your mother."

She gasped and stepped back. "That's not true. Here you go with your rumors again."

He grabbed her shoulders so she couldn't run, which struck him as funny, because he'd been the one to run.

"It's true, Brie. The night before our wedding, I was nervous and went looking for Dad to talk to. I'd thought my parents were lucky at love since they'd been married forever, but all I ever saw was the time they spent together. I never saw what their marriage was like when I wasn't around."

"You have it wrong. My father loved my mother."

He nodded. "That may be true, but your mother loved my father. Reread the letter with the information you now have."

"It's not true." She escaped his grasp. "You're making it up."

"I wish I were, but I saw it. I walked into the boathouse and found them together—intimately."

"How can you say that?"

"Brie, it's why I ran. How was I supposed to stand at the altar with Dad at my side as my best man? Everything I knew about my life changed that day. Everything I believed about love was lost. How was I supposed to look at you and talk about love and forever without telling you our parents were living the biggest lie of all? Knowing what I knew, how was I supposed to shake hands with your father? If I had told you, you wouldn't have believed me. I was willing to let you hate me, but I refused to let you hate them. You believed they had perfect love. I wasn't about to ruin that for you. You'd get over me, but I wasn't sure you'd get over the truth."

She hugged the book as a tear rolled down her cheek. "I don't believe you."

"That's what I expected twelve years ago. Can't you see how impossible the situation was? You're not the twenty-year-old girl you were then. You're a grown woman, and you still can't fathom it. Can you see why I did what I did?"

"They're dead and can't defend themselves. How dare you?"

"It's the truth. Go ask Em."

Brie started to hyperventilate. "No... it... can't be true." He moved toward her, but she held up a hand as a stop sign. "You're a liar. You're lying."

"I never lied. I just didn't tell you the truth. I couldn't. But Brie, that's all in the past. Can't we forget about it and focus on the future?"

"We have no future if we lie to each other." She pushed past him and ran.

TWENTY-SEVEN

Brie went to Tilly's kitchen. At times like this, a broken heart needed coffee and sweets—lots of sweets. At this hour she expected to see a skeleton crew, but it was as busy as a beehive. She skated the perimeter and sat at a table loaded with goodies as if they were waiting for her.

"I thought you'd be in," Tilly said.

Brie jumped at the sound of her voice and spun to face her. "How did you know?"

"Are those tears? You can't be crying now. You're finally getting everything you wanted."

The floodgates opened. She threw herself in Tilly's arms. "Everything is ruined."

Tilly finished the hug and then went straight to the coffeepot to pour two cups. "I assure you everything is on schedule. The cake will be finished tomorrow, and a full staff is working overtime to prep the food. You don't have to worry about a thing."

Brie shook her head. "How am I supposed to marry a man I can't trust?"

Tilly picked up a rolling pin. "If that boy ran again, I'm going to beat the ever-lovin' hell out of him."

Brie hung her head. "He didn't run, I did."

"Oh honey, it's just cold feet." Tilly sat beside her and passed the plate of sweets. "Grab something, and let's talk about it. Shall I call Em? She's always good at giving advice."

"No!" Brie shook her head so hard, she thought she'd scrambled her brain. "She's part of the problem." She pointed to the books she'd set on the table. "Carter claims my mother was having an affair with his father. Why would he say such a thing?" She pulled the letter from her pocket and set it on the table. "He says this is a love letter from Cyrus to Mom."

She expected Tilly to read the letter, but she didn't. She looked at Brie with sad eyes. "I'm sorry you had to find out like that."

Brie narrowed her eyes. "You too? Are you saying it's true?"

Tilly exhaled. "I'm not saying it isn't." It was Tilly's diplomatic answer to a tough question.

"How many other people know?"

Tilly stuck a whole cookie in her mouth, like a kid avoiding answering the question.

"I'll wait until you swallow." Tilly did but immediately picked up a new cookie. Brie snatched it from her. "Tell me."

"This is a family matter. You should talk to your aunt."

If Tilly wanted Aunt Em to confirm, then it was true. "I've known you all my life, and that makes you family. How long did the affair go on? Was she sleeping with Cyrus for years or was it a quick fling?"

"They were like you and Carter."

As if mentioning his name had summoned him, he appeared, but Brie held up her hand. "I'm not ready to talk to you. You lied to me." She looked at Tilly. "You lied to me, too. It seems the entire town has been lying to me. Who am I supposed to trust?" She buried her head in her hands and wept.

"Were we lying to you or protecting you?" Carter asked.

Brie's head snapped up. "How was that protecting me? You were protecting them. All this time, you kept this secret." She gasped and covered her mouth. "Oh my god, you let me go on and on about my parents' pure love and the perfection of their relationship when you knew Mom was cheating on Dad." She turned to Tilly. "And you knew it all along. Aren't you ashamed of yourself?"

"It wasn't my truth to tell or my cross to bear."

Brie pointed at Carter. "Instead of being honest with me, you just didn't show up at our wedding. Who does that? And what about my poor father? He truly loved my mother, and she did him wrong."

Carter said, "Nothing about you has changed. You have more information about your family, but who you are remains the same. Who we are together remains unchanged. I'm still the man who loves you and wants to spend his life with you."

"Tilly said our parents were like you and me. What does that mean?"

Carter and Tilly exchanged glances, but it was Carter who spoke. "From what I can gather, they were born for each other, but their families forbade the romance. They were a cross between Romeo and Juliet and Prince Charles and Camilla. Madly in love but couldn't pursue the relationship because, like the Montagues, there was a family feud. But like Prince Charles and Camilla, they figured out how to give everyone what they wanted and still get what they needed in stolen moments."

Brie sat in silence with her hand on the heart-embossed journals. "But did anyone get what they wanted?" Her eyes widened. "What if I'm your half-sister?" She looked like she might be sick.

Carter adamantly shook his head. "That was part of my fear the night I found them together, but my mother told me she knew for certain you were Benton's. And look at you. You have his nose and hair."

She nodded in agreement. "Did my mom know why you ran?"

"No."

"I guess there's that. She was obviously selfish, but at least she didn't ruin my life on purpose and then pretend afterward she didn't know." She tucked the letter into the journal. "Did my father know about the affair?"

Carter nodded. "Your father died on a boat full of half-naked coeds. He wasn't a saint either."

"What about Claudia?"

"She knew but undervalued herself. It wasn't until you and I left that she felt the loneliness and moved on."

Brie picked up the books and stood. "I need time to process this."

"How much time?"

She knew what he was asking without actually asking. Would she be there the day after tomorrow to marry him?

"I don't know." That was the answer to everything. She wasn't sure how much time she'd need to get over the betrayal. She wasn't sure if she could. She needed to confront her aunt, and by the time she arrived at the private residence, Em was waiting. "How could you?"

Em said nothing. She stepped aside and closed the door, then put on the instant kettle to boil and set two teacups on the kitchen counter.

"I didn't sleep with Cyrus, so stop blaming me." She measured loose leaf tea into baskets and set them in the floral China cups while waiting for the water to boil. "I know a lot of things I don't tell others."

"But this is personal."

The water boiled and Em poured it into the waiting cups. She delivered them to the table, where they both sat.

"Everything is personal to someone. This was personal to your mother and Cyrus and Benton and Claudia."

"And me?"

Em briefly closed her eyes. "It's only personal because you feel you weren't in on the secret, but the clues were around you all the time."

"Oh no, they weren't." She yanked the letter out of the journal. "I knew nothing until I found this. You knew it was there, and you gave me these, hoping I'd find them. You told me they were recipe and gardening journals."

Em raised her brows. "They aren't?"

Brie didn't really know because she hadn't gone through them. She opened the top one, and on the first page was a drawing of the gardens around the resort. As she turned the pages, she saw it was a book on gardening, but hidden in the pictures were tiny messages, like the one written beside a rose-bush. *I'll love you forever* was penned in her mother's neat hand-writing.

She opened the twin book and in it was a picture of The Kessler Resort. In less than perfect script was a similar inscription that read *I'm counting on that,* placed next to a crude drawing of flowers. Over the years they'd exchanged journals and written secret messages in the drawings. She imagined her mother leaving hers on the dock rail, only to have Cyrus swing by and switch them. Then her mother could claim she'd forgotten it and run down to pick it up.

"They are, but they're more." She pointed to the scribblings and then closed the book. "You didn't know when you gave them to me?"

Em smiled. "I'm not a gardener or a cook, so I didn't even look."

"Were they really in love all their lives?"

Em sipped her tea. "Since the day they met, but there was tension between the families and your grandparents were strict. We weren't allowed to date outside our circle, and the Kesslers weren't in our circle."

"It wasn't financial. They had a resort too."

Em shrugged. "It's all perception. There's five-star lodging and motels. Both have beds to sleep in, but you wouldn't call them the same. The Browns have always been quality. We were like old money in this town, and the Kesslers weren't, but they thought they were equals. Grandpa Brown made sure they could never keep up. Good enough never was, and there wasn't anyone good enough for his girls."

"Why Daddy?" Brie asked.

"Because he was controllable. Your father was kind and a pushover, which in the end, worked out for your mother and Cyrus. Same with Claudia. Both had to know what was happening, but they didn't have the backbone to stop it, so Cyrus and your mother carried on for years."

"I wish you would have told me."

Em placed her hand on Brie's. "I accidentally did the night I was drunk, but it went over your head. Would knowing have changed anything?"

She wondered if it would have helped or hurt her. Had she known, would she have hated Cyrus for interfering in her life? Would that have changed her relationship with Carter? If Carter hadn't known, would he have felt the same for her? "He left me on our wedding day."

"He did but consider this. You're thirty-two and you're having a hard time processing it. Imagine being twenty and walking in on it." Em finished her tea. "Now that you know, what are you going to do? Will you get married, or will you run?"

Nothing had changed, and yet everything had changed. "I need time to figure it out."

Em rose and put her cup in the sink. "Time isn't a luxury you have. There's a wedding in about thirty-six hours." She kissed Brie's forehead. "You can take the guest room upstairs. While you're pondering your future, all I ask is you consider the past. He gave you up because he wanted to protect you and preserve the life you thought you had. Will you give him up and ruin the life you can create together? Haven't the Browns and Kesslers sacrificed enough?"

Brie followed her aunt upstairs to the spare room. It had once belonged to her, but unlike Carter's room, it wasn't a shrine to her past. Every bit of her had been wiped clean. Maybe it was better that way. She wasn't the girl who'd fallen asleep in this room, dreaming of unicorns and rainbows and Carter's kisses. She was a woman who'd experienced trials and tragedy and survived them all. Losing Carter had been the death of every schoolgirl dream she'd had. She dozed off to a question: Did she hold on to the past or move on with her future?

WHEN BRIE WOKE MID-MORNING, there wasn't a sound in the house, which meant Aunt Em was already manning the front desk. Many questions still ran through her head. At times like this, she would have gone to her mom for counsel, like she'd done that tragic day when her life fell apart. Her mother had held her and wiped her tears. Carter said Olivia hadn't known Carter had walked in on them, but over the years, she must have suspected. And still, she continued her affair with Cyrus, as evidenced by Claudia leaving and her father, Benton, carrying on with other women. Cyrus had to know. Carter had abandoned Willow Bay, whereas Brie had left but stayed in touch with her parents. It was all so confusing. Last night it had been a betrayal. Today it was a tragedy. Many lives had been ruined because two old codgers couldn't meet in the middle. Or maybe it went back to her grandfather being so rigid. Was that what had happened to Aunt Em and Miles?

Her stomach growled, but she wasn't ready to face anyone at the resort, so she showered, borrowed a fresh outfit from Aunt Em's closet, and went to Cricket's. She was the wisest woman Brie knew.

She lucked out with a parking place in front and stepped inside the diner. She breathed in bacon and coffee. Who didn't love the smell of breakfast?

"Sit down. I've been expecting you."

"You have?"

Cricket brought over a carafe of coffee and sat across from her. "Carter called and said you might be coming this way. Your pancakes are cooking, and Sam is making that bacon extra crispy, the way you like it."

"Thank you."

"Don't thank me. Thank that man of yours. He's looking after you." She poured them coffee. "What's this I hear about you running?"

Brie's mouth dropped open. "Did he tell you that?"

"That was Tilly. She wanted me to talk some sense into you."

Brie sipped her coffee. "Did you know about our parents?"

"I did."

"I feel like an idiot. I'm the only one who didn't know. It was all there, but I never saw what was in front of me."

Cricket smiled. "If you've come for my advice, you're making this too easy."

Brie hated that she was so transparent. "What am I supposed to do about everything I know? I'm surrounded by people who lied to me. How can I marry a man who left me years ago because he thought he knew better than me?"

"Was he right about you not believing him then? Do you believe him now?"

Cricket glanced over her shoulder at the order window and rose to get the plate waiting there. When she returned, she set Brie's breakfast down. "While you digest this, I'd like you to chew on something else. Go back to the resort and look around. Take it all in. Now that your eyes are open, maybe you'll see things more clearly. When you're finished, think about your future. How do you picture it? Love is not your problem, perspective is." Cricket started off. "I might need to write that down and sell it. I think this deserves a big tip, don't you?"

Brie laughed. "The biggest."

As she ate, she let Cricket's words sink in, only she amended them. Love wasn't her problem. Trust was. Could she trust her gut? Her mind? Her heart? Now that her eyes were finally open, what would she see?

"OPEN MY EYES," Brie said as she parked the car at the resort. "What am I supposed to see?" She noticed lots of people on the beach. Normally she wouldn't pay much attention, but she was curious about whether she'd missed something. Families played with their children. A young couple sat with their toddler near the water and built a sandcastle.

"That's lovely," Brie said.

The woman perked up. "Could you take a picture? We do this every year, and I want to remember it."

"Sure." Brie took the woman's phone and moved back to snap the picture. "You come to The Brown Resort every year?"

"This is our first year here. We usually stay at The Kessler, but this year they were closed, so we reserved a bungalow at The Brown."

"Great. How's your stay going?"

"It's wonderful. We miss Mr. Kessler. I hope he's okay."

She could have pretended she knew nothing but wasn't that what had hurt her? People knew things and didn't share. "Mr. Kessler died, but his son is taking over, so before you leave, you can talk to Margot at the front desk and reserve for next year."

"That's sad. He was so kind."

Brie nodded. "He was a good man." Miraculously, she meant it. Cyrus had always been kind to her. She realized she hadn't introduced herself. "I'm Brie, and my family owns The Brown, but my fiancé Carter is Mr. Kessler's son and now owns The Kessler."

The woman looked at her. "I'm Mia, and that's so cool to be rival resorts and maintain close family connections."

Cool wasn't the word she would have chosen, but in hindsight, it wasn't the worst thing for her mother and Cyrus to have had a connection. Without it, the family feud would still be going.

"If you need anything, don't be afraid to ask." Brie returned the phone and went to The Kessler boathouse. Carter had roped it off, but she ducked under and went to the door. When she looked up, she saw where they'd etched their initials and a heart into the wood. They'd been only fourteen, but they were already in love. By the doorjamb was a faded etching she hadn't noticed before because it had been beaten bare by the elements, but if she looked closely, it was a C and an O intertwined. She rubbed the indentation.

"Those are all over the place," Claudia said beside her.

Brie hadn't heard her approach. "I'm sorry about the letter. I didn't know."

Claudia embraced Brie. "How could you?"

She pointed to the initials. "How could I not? It's all over both resorts." She thought back to the engraving on the tree. "Some of these are so worn, they looked like two Cs. I always thought it was a romantic gesture that you and Cyrus carved your love into every-thing. It's why Carter and I did."

"It was a romantic gesture, but not for me. Those are the carv-ings of two teens in a forbidden love. From what Cyrus told me, they carved their initials everywhere, so even if they couldn't be together, they'd know the other's love existed."

"It must have been hell for you, seeing it all the time."

"I always thought I could make him forget her."

"But she lived next door."

"There was that." She laughed. "Just so you know, Cyrus was good to me."

"How can you say that? He cheated on you."

"I used to think of it that way, but by marrying me, he cheated on your mother. They should have been together all along. They were connected on a deep level. No one should have stood in their way."

"I'm sorry you had to go through that."

"I'm sorry you had to go through what you went through but let me ask you something."

"Anything."

"If you could go back in time, would you give up your life with David to have Carter from the beginning?"

The thought of not having David in her life hurt. "No. I learned so much from him. My time with David helped mold me into the woman I am today. I think I'd be less without him."

Claudia touched Brie's shoulders. "I feel the same way about Cyrus. He couldn't give me the love I needed because his heart belonged to another. Despite that, he was the best man he could be. I wanted what he and your mom had, and I found it with Frank. Sometimes you get the love you're destined for right out of the gate, and sometimes there are lessons to be learned first." She smiled. "I'm a better wife to Frank because of what I learned in my marriage to Cyrus. I paid my dues, and I earned Frank."

"Yes, you did."

The two women hugged.

"I know you don't understand why no one told you, but what good would it have done? There are reasons why they don't let kids drive until a certain age and sex education is taught in a particular grade. You're not ready for the responsibility. With infidelity in parents... kids are never ready for that. All they need to know is, no matter what, their parents love them."

Claudia was right. Brie had been angry everyone had lied to her, but that wasn't the truth. No one had lied to her. They'd just kept the dirty truth to themselves. "Thank you for the talk."

"Of course, sweetie. Can I give you some advice?"

Brie was all about getting advice today and nodded.

"You and Carter are like Cyrus and Olivia. You have a pure love that can't be broken. No matter what happens in your life, you will always love each other. Think about how that looks for your future. Don't be the ones who love from afar. Long distance, even next door, never works. You have a second chance, and if you have doubts, let love decide." She kissed Brie on the cheek. "Go pamper yourself. Tomorrow you'll be a bride."

"What if this isn't the right time?" So many things had

happened that she had to wonder if the universe was giving her a message.

"There's never a wrong time for love."

Brie returned to her room, Claudia's words running through her head. Could a person ever love too much, too long, or too hard?

TWENTY-EIGHT

"Stop pacing like a trapped animal," Claudia said as she ironed his shirt. "She'll show up."

"Mom, the wedding is less than an hour away. Except for the *I love you* text she sent, she hasn't spoken to me since the night everything came to a head."

Frank set a hand on his shoulder. "That message was like a promise. No one says 'I love you' and doesn't show up at their wedding." Carter stared at Frank long and hard. "Okay, you did, but she's not you. She'll show."

His mother kissed him on the cheek and stood back. "I spoke to her yesterday. She was reflecting on life and love."

"Did she say anything that would make you believe she didn't want to marry me?"

"No." She pointed to the window. Outside, staff bustled about, putting flowers on tables, and guests moseyed about the property. "Does that look like she's not going to show?"

"I saw two women enter the house an hour ago," Frank said. "One looked ready for church and the other for war."

"Honey, you're not helping. Why don't you get us a drink? Soda for me, and maybe something stronger for Carter."

"Mom, it's not even ten."

She giggled. "You're right, but a little shot in your coffee might calm your nerves."

"My nerves are fine. It's my heart that aches." Marybeth and Charlotte being there was a good sign. Or was it? It could go both ways. They could be there to help her get ready or pick up the pieces. What he wanted was to see Brie, but he knew the rules. A man didn't get to see his bride before the wedding.

Frank returned with two cups of coffee, a soda, and a small bottle of whiskey. "I saw the groom's cake. It's shaped like a hammer, and Em sends her regards."

"Em was there?" He took his freshly ironed shirt from the hanger and put it on. "I'll be right back." Before his mother could stop him, he rushed out the door to the lobby, only to find Em gone. His shoulders slumped forward as he turned and walked straight into Margot. "Sorry."

She looked at him like he was melting ice cream she wanted to lick. "Just the man I'm looking for. You do look delicious."

If Margot was going to be a permanent part of their staff, she'd need some training. Did they accept thirty-year-olds in Miss Manners classes? "What did you need?"

Margot smiled and looked at a note in her hand. "I was told to deliver this."

His heart sunk. Was it a Dear John letter? "Who's it from?"

She smiled. "I can't say. I can only say that time's wasting. Every girl wants to look down the aisle and see the expression on her man's face. You don't want to miss that twice." She pointed to the note. "So, figure that out."

He crossed the lobby and went outside where he opened the letter.

Carter,
Come to Em's, we need to talk.
Brie

He clutched the paper in his hand and rushed around the back of the resort to where Em's house stood. She was waiting at the door.

"What's going on?"

She shrugged and pointed upstairs. "I can't say, but Brie wants to talk to you."

"Isn't that bad luck?" Part of him wanted to turn and run again. Not away but to the willow tree where he promised to wait for her. At least there he had hope they would marry and live happily ever after. But right now, he wasn't sure. She summoned him for a reason and considering how they'd left things, the prospects of a wedding seemed slim.

"I don't believe in luck. I believe in action," Em said. "Now get up there and see what she wants. I can promise you one thing. There's no chance of a wedding if you don't go."

Carter took the stairs one at a time. It felt like a death march. When he got to the top, he knocked, and Brie opened the door. She was dressed in a robe and had her hair wrapped in a towel. It wasn't how he'd imagined her to be, but at this point, he was happy to see her.

"Can I hug you?"

She nodded, and he pulled her into his arms and hugged her like the lifeline she was. When he pulled away, he took her in. "When we said casual, this wasn't what I'd envisioned, but I like it."

She chuckled. "I'm not ready."

His heart tumbled until he was sure it fell to the floor and stubbed his toe. He dropped to his knees. "That's okay. We can postpone. I don't care. All I care about is you."

She smiled. "I appreciate that, but I meant, I'm not ready to put my dress on. Charlotte is downstairs pacing the floors and Marybeth is praying for us, but I said I couldn't in my right mind marry you until we talked."

He moved her words through his head like a puzzle. "Does that mean you're going to marry me?"

He rose, and she took his hand and led him to her bed where they sat looking at each other. "I can't start our marriage on lies and misunderstandings. We need to start without heavy hearts. I'm sorry you didn't feel like you could talk to me all those years ago. I apologize for looking around and never seeing the truth."

"Brie, I didn't see either until I actually saw."

She held up her hand. "I'm mostly sorry I didn't have the maturity to deal with the problem. You were right to leave, but it breaks my heart that you had to bear the sadness and loss alone. As your partner, I should have been there for you."

He tapped his chest. "You were always right here, baby." He held both her hands. "I'm sorry I ran. The funny thing is, I kept running and look where I ended up—back here with you. It's because this is where I belong."

"And I with you." She leaned forward and pressed her forehead to his. "Are we good?"

He cupped her cheek. "Better than good."

She rose and pointed to the door. "Then get out of my room. You're not supposed to see the bride before you marry her."

"Yes, ma'am. Can I have a kiss before I go?"

She shook her head. "No way mister, there's got to be something you're looking forward to."

"Oh, I am. There's tonight and the honeymoon. But mostly I'm looking forward to forever with you."

She walked him to the door. "Don't get lost on your way to our tree."

He snuck a kiss to her cheek. "I'll be there waiting."

He left her room feeling light and free and happy. He walked outside where he saw dozens of cloth-draped tables decorated with vases of Brie's favorite flowers on the beach. Servers stood ready in case a guest needed something. Pastor Davidson was walking down the walkway toward the willow tree with his bible in hand. Claudia was there, waiting for him. He'd asked her to be his best woman. He'd had a moment of regret for not mending fences with his father. Life rarely gave a person a do-over, but he'd been granted that blessing with Brie, and he was grateful. He took a deep breath and let it out slowly. Walking confidently down the aisle between a hundred filled chairs, he took his place beside his mother.

"This is really happening," he said with awe.

"Yes, honey. The world is righting a wrong."

He waited for what seemed like a lifetime before a violinist stood and played what he recognized as Pachelbel's Canon in D Major. It was the song Brie had always wanted when she walked down the aisle. The guests fell silent and waited. Moments later, Brie appeared next to her aunt in a gorgeous flowing white sundress. She wore a crown of flowers and held a bouquet of her favorite flowers. When she drew near, he looked into her eyes and saw only love.

Em presented her to him, and they faced each other. "Best day of my life," he whispered, kissing her cheek.

"This is where I'm supposed to be."

Pastor Davidson cleared his throat. "We are gathered here..."

The ceremony wasn't long. They hadn't wanted something lengthy, they just wanted to be married. As they repeated their vows and promised to see each other through thick and thin, they could hardly wait to be married. Finally, he said the words they'd been waiting to hear. "You can kiss your bride."

As Carter leaned in to do that, Brie held up a finger. "Wait a second." Even the birds stopped chirping. Everyone held their breath. "I have a few words for my almost-husband."

Pastor Davidson said, "This isn't the time for a pre-nuptial agreement."

"Let her speak," Carter said.

Brie took both his hands in hers. "What's mine is mine, and what's yours is mine."

The crowd laughed, and someone said, "That's a southern girl for you."

"Anything you want," he said. "You stole my heart, and everything else comes with it."

"We are equals," she added.

The men sitting in the crowd grumbled, but Carter's value wasn't tied up in his ego. "We are."

"Okay then, what's yours is yours, and what's mine is yours. No more secrets. No more lies."

"I agree, and I'm sorry."

She looked at him as if they were the only two people who existed. "It wasn't your secret to tell. And it isn't mine to carry. Now that's resolved, you may kiss your bride."

Pastor Davidson laughed. "That's my line."

Neither paid attention as he announced they were officially husband and wife because they were lost in the kiss.

THE FIRST TO GREET THEM in the reception line was Tiffany, who threw herself into Brie's arms. "I told you I'd make it to the resort." She pointed to the table where gifts were stacked three high. "I brought you a lifetime of sweets, but you won't need them. You married the sweetest man around."

"I did," Brie said and gazed at Carter like the sun rose and set in his eyes.

They greeted their guests, and as the last person approached, Carter glimpsed Brie's shoes—bedazzled sneakers—and smiled. "Did you wear those in case you ran?"

"Silly man, these are for dancing. If I were to run, I wouldn't have bedazzled them. The sequins would have left a trail for you to find me."

"I would have found you."

"I wouldn't have run too far."

THE NEXT AFTERNOON, they were packed and ready for their honeymoon. Aunt Em joined them at Carter's truck to say farewell.

"Don't worry about The Kessler. I'll make sure everything runs smoothly."

Brie looked at him as if to say, *Should we tell her?* "In all the commotion, we forgot to tell you we hired a general manager."

Em cocked her head in confusion. "You what?"

"We hired a general manager. We've watched and learned and don't want to be married to the resort. We want to be married to each other."

"Who did you hire?"

Tires on gravel drew their attention, and Miles parked and stepped out of his truck.

"You remember Miles, right?"

"You've got to be kidding me. Why would you do that?"

Brie touched her aunt's arm. "You asked me to come here to help you." She pointed to Miles. "I'm up to the task, Aunt Em. We'll see you when we get back."

Carter opened the door for his wife. He handed the resort keys to Miles in passing and turned to Em. "It would be great if you could make Miles feel welcome."

Em opened and closed her mouth several times. "But."

"As a wedding gift to me?" Brie asked. "After everything, it's really the least you can do."

Em frowned and nodded. Carter climbed into the truck and drove away. In the rearview mirror, he watched the two circle each other like boxers in a ring. "This should be interesting. Do you think there will be anything left when we get home?"

"We'll have to see." She reached for his hand, and as they drove away from Willow Bay, this time they knew they'd be back.

Find out what happens with Emmaline and Miles in *Here With You*.

Do you love a good southern recipe? Download The Recipes of Willow Bay here.

OTHER BOOKS BY KELLY COLLINS

Willow Bay

The Second Time Around

Here With You

An Aspen Cove Romance Series

One Hundred Reasons

One Hundred Heartbeats

One Hundred Wishes

One Hundred Promises

One Hundred Excuses

One Hundred Christmas Kisses

One Hundred Lifetimes

One Hundred Ways

One Hundred Goodbyes

One Hundred Secrets

One Hundred Regrets

One Hundred Choices

One Hundred Decisions

One Hundred Glances

One Hundred Lessons

One Hundred Mistakes

One Hundred Nights

One Hundred Whispers
One Hundred Reflections
One Hundred Chances

JOIN MY READER'S CLUB AND GET A FREE BOOK.

Go to www.authorkellycollins.com

ABOUT THE AUTHOR

International bestselling author of more than thirty novels, Kelly Collins writes with the intention of keeping love alive. Always a romantic, she blends real-life events with her vivid imagination to create characters and stories that lovers of contemporary romance, new adult, and romantic suspense will return to again and again.

For More Information
www.authorkellycollins.com
kelly@authorkellycollins.com

CPSIA information can be obtained
at www.ICGtesting.com
Printed in the USA
BVHW051335080223
658130BV00015B/407